MONTGOMERY
STREET

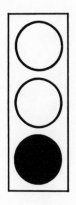

MONTGOMERY STREET

A NOVEL

BY *Mark Dintenfass*

1817 **HARPER & ROW, PUBLISHERS**

NEW YORK, HAGERSTOWN, SAN FRANCISCO, LONDON

MONTGOMERY STREET. Copyright © 1978 by Mark Dintenfass. All rights reserved. Printed in the United States of America. No part of this book may be used or reproduced in any manner whatsoever without written permission except in the case of brief quotations embodied in critical articles and reviews. For information address Harper & Row, Publishers, Inc., 10 East 53rd Street, New York, N.Y. 10022. Published simultaneously in Canada by Fitzhenry & Whiteside Limited, Toronto.

FIRST EDITION

Designed by Sidney Feinberg

Library of Congress Cataloging in Publication Data

Dintenfass, Mark.
  Montgomery Street.
  I. Title.
PZ4.D586Mo   [PS3554.I5]   813'.5'4   77-11785
ISBN 0-06-011063-5

78 79 80 81 82 10 9 8 7 6 5 4 3 2 1

For Nathan

MONTGOMERY STREET

The Films of Stephen Mandreg

   Neighbors, 1964 (37 minutes)

   Night and Early Morning, 1965 (12 minutes)

   Tree, 1965 (8 minutes)

   Welcome to Sugarloaf, 1969 (11 minutes)

   This Old Man, 1970 (a "semi-documentary," 89 minutes)

   Porkpie, 1971 (unreleased, 170 minutes)

   Centerpiece,* 1976 (96 minutes)

   Montgomery Street, 1977 (101 minutes)

PREFACE

There is, of course, in the "real" world a "real" Montgomery Street. It originates at the western edge of the Brooklyn Botanic Garden and runs due east, without deviation, past the ghost of Ebbets Field, through the heart of Crown Heights, and on toward the squalor and despair of Brownsville. I have not seen that Montgomery Street for ten years, and I suspect it looks nothing at all like the Montgomery Street depicted in the movie called Montgomery Street, *the latter being an illusory sort of place concocted from scraps of other streets in distant neighborhoods, and populated by professional mimics and rented vintage cars. Every creation must disappoint its maker; nothing ever turns out quite the way it was foreseen in the shadowland of expectation. In an ideal world, where imaginings could be projected straight onto a screen, or better yet, waft from mind to mind without the mediation of our unreliable senses, there would be still a third Montgomery Street, the one that meanders through my memories and suffuses my dreams. That third Montgomery Street—along with the interest aroused by the success of the movie, the desire of interviewers and enthusiasts to probe the so-called "source" of my so-called "inspiration"—provides the reason for this book.*

It is my practice to "conceive" a movie bit by bit on

paper, to try to see the thing in the round, so to speak, long before a script is written, a contract signed. It's a kind of play (I almost said foreplay) that, for me, must precede the actual labors of movie-making, and it matters not at all that a character who looms large in the "notes" (Max, for example) dwindles to a mere turn or two in the finished film, or that some sequence everyone loves (such as Ellie's frantic afternoon) came as an afterthought, improvised on location. I offer this, incidentally, merely by way of explanation; against those critics who berate me for being too "bookish," too much a creature of words, there is no useful defense.

These pages, anyway, were accumulated during three months of bemused and occasionally joyous scribbling in the summer and autumn of 1976. I have suppressed a few irrelevancies, regularized my punctuation, and fleshed out a few otherwise indecipherable passages, all for the sake of readability; but I have tried to keep them spiritually intact. I hope they are informative; I hope they are entertaining. My editor tells me that for him the story of the creation of Montgomery Street *is more "fascinating" than the movie itself. But he is, perhaps, too kind. And when he goes on to suggest that my "notes" say something "significant" about the "role of the American artist," well, I can only smile and try to seem appropriately inscrutable. I do not, to be candid, believe in "significance" or in that ponderous and romantic rigmarole called "art." I am merely a craftsman, a lover of form and process and prerequisite skill, happy enough to exist from time to time in a basically simple realm where action meets film and film meets mind and pleasure is occasionally achieved. It is the sharing of that pleasure with readers and film-lovers that, finally, justifies these "notes."*

Stephen Mandreg
Sète, France, 1977

For both art and life depend wholly
on the laws of optics, on perspective and illusion;
both, to be blunt, depend on the necessity of error.

NIETZSCHE

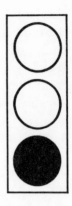

My day in the sun. Screenings, shoptalk, exotic women, exhibitionists, whirling crowds, too many cigarettes, a permanent smile . . . I suppose I can look forward to a sleepless night. Success in this business, maybe any success, can be measured by the number of people who try to touch you. It's a fondling sort of thing, as though they think the magic might rub off, that they can nip a piece of it for themselves. They grab your hand, they squeeze your elbow, they pummel your back. An Italian producer (never got his name) threw a heavy arm around my neck and breathed corruption into my face. A woman with pink hair slipped her key into my pocket and I had to send Mort around to give it back. And every time I turned my head there was Z beaming at his fair-haired boy. So I've happened. I've had a whiff of power and freedom, for a moment I own the world. But I'm also feeling bruised and cautious, and a bit rancid under the

1

arms. All over Cannes this week you see former boy wonders, one-time geniuses, names you used to know. Now they can only skulk and fawn and wait, they've become their own clichés. Which is why through it all, the banquets and toasts, the promotions, the interviews, the parties, the hullabaloo, I keep thinking: what do I do for an encore, where do I go from here?

———

A movie about a man making a movie, the process itself, the multiple takes, the story line slowly emerging, having to go back and rethink a scene because what looked so fine on paper just won't film. The play of it, the work of it. The childishness of performers, the camaraderie of the crew, hassles with the producer, the usual game. How images never match up to reality. How community springs up around a single dream. The filmmaker on a set, a great fat spider in the midst of his web. The pressures on him. The way he becomes obsessed with his own visions. His stubborn integrity. His—

Sure, sure, why not—and the beautiful actress who adores him. Hi there, Fellini! Howdy, Truffaut!

The universal wolf devouring itself, all bloody entrails and rank silvery fur.

———

Slipped out of a screening (revolutionary epic by some hot-eyed Greek), set off to explore the town a bit, and ran into Georgie Kaplan, of all people. He's gone bald and pink and fat over the years but there was no mistaking him. We stood in the sun like a couple of old cellmates and chatted in Brooklynese. He's in real estate, he's married, he produced snapshots of a kid, he told a pointless story about his father's death. Same old George. Which made me feel I wasn't quite the same old Stevie. I hardly recognize myself here, anyway not in Georgie's eyes. When he asked me what I was doing in Cannes my face began to burn. Somehow the festival and the success of *Centerpiece* began to seem like a shameful secret. I found myself mouthing to this

Montgomery Street ghost some nonsense about being in the "entertainment racket," and then, not very gracefully, I made my escape. Swam back to the hotel through a turbulence of memories. Now my ears are ringing, my head aches, I feel myself getting frantic, last year all over again. If I don't get back to work soon, I may lose everything.

———

Signing an autograph, you feel a bit like some African tribesman photographed by a tourist, afraid they've stolen your soul.

———

Everyone here has a project to peddle. Treatments and scripts come in the mail; story ideas are thrust into your hand. Mort says I should read some of this stuff, see what other people are up to. Okay, what are other people up to? Mostly murder, of course. They all seem to think their angry fantasies should pile up literal corpses on the screen. Rape movies, revenge movies, assassin movies, disaster movies, devil movies, chillers, thrillers, all with some new angle, but seldom a trace of humor in any of it. Will there ever again be an American movie that is not garish, bloody, or maudlin, a film that is more than a funhouse mirror? How juvenile really is that urge to shock. Movies are dreams, sure, but dreams if they're to touch us must be concocted of the stuff of lives—sights, sounds, moods, memories. The interesting murders in this world are hidden, mental, oblique.

A movie in that?

———

Lunch with Z. A haze of friendship and good cheer around a core that was all business. What's your next project? he wants to know. Told him I needed a few more weeks before I'd be ready to talk about it. He pushed a bit; I balked. He talked about the success syndrome. We ate strawberries for dessert. He mentioned an unpublished novel he's taken an option on. I didn't ask to read it. Think of something soon or he'll have me up to my neck in blood and gore. Or worse, another *Centerpiece*.

A man finds a gun. It terrifies him. What will he do with it?

Something simple. A day in the life of. The impulse is to outdo myself, which is why I've been stuck. Easy set-ups, basic lighting, plain cuts. You don't have to dazzle them. Trust yourself.

Poor Mort. The look on his face when I said I was leaving, didn't know my destination, would be in touch. Mort was mortified. What about the interview with *Der Spiegel*, what about Z's reception? Tell Z I've become eccentric, I said. He'll be impressed.

Drove all day. The ride in a rented Renault was invigorating. Lunch in Marseilles, dinner in Sète. It's a fishing town on the road to Spain, a homey sort of place where people seem to work for a living, and not just the waiters and whores. The French show up here for a beach holiday with their kids. I feel as though I've passed back through the looking glass, back to gray reality. Already my head seems clearer. It's the kind of place you could film in black and white, and not miss much. Think I'll stay a while, see what comes. I'm free and single and money's rolling in. Might as well make the most of it.

Swam, ate, walked an hour along the shore. It's more Brighton Beach than Fire Island here. Pizza stands, cheap restaurants, teen-agers with towels rolled up under their arms. The hotel serves a pretty peach melba with soft ice cream out of a machine. Saw a sight: a busload of Germans en route to the Costa Brava stopped beachside, and all the old ladies climbed down kvetching, hitched up their skirts, and went strolling in the surf. *Schön, schön.* Reminded me, of course, of the neighbors on Montgomery Street. The sun on my back was a balm for my spirit. There was a pretty girl on a motorcycle, kids at play. Some men with a

4

bulldozer were pulling a dredging net filled with fish and mussels and squid and muck out of the ocean; then they had to wade in to sort the mess out. Yellow hip boots, blue sweaters: framed and filed. My eyes are beginning to work again.

———

Mort on the phone: Z is peeved. He knows damn well I have nothing in mind, and says when I go off to work alone I tend to get "European." "Art is a film that dies in Manhattan." And it's all true. My mind's blank, I can't really shake the mood. What is it? Homesick? Missing E, the kids? Residue of last year's down? No, I'm not lonely, not that lonely anyway. I'm just not quite used to being alone. Which is why I'm so reluctant to go back to New York, I suppose. My glum apartment, my optimistic double bed. Some swinger I am.

I suppose I can always go back to Cannes and enjoy my bit of celebrity. In this town I'm just another sloppy American, French-less and grim. I keep having the miserable desire to stop people on the street and tell them, look, I'm somebody, I make movies, I'm famous. Can't win. I suppose all I really want is to be working again. What a nonsensical Puritan I am, always will be. Never mind. I can hope, anyway, that these inklings of gloom are just a prelude to inspiration.

———

Take stock: because *Centerpiece* is going to gross twenty million dollars (says Mort) I'm as free as anyone ever gets in this business to make the movie I want. Okay, what sort of movie do I want? Another fancy sex comedy, which is all *Centerpiece* really is? That movie about making movies, a bit of pseudo Truffaut? A man finding a gun? What man? Where? When? The freedom itself seems to be the problem. Because asking what sort of movie I want is the same as asking what do I think, what do I feel, what manner of man have I become—and that's where I start going in circles. Is that really me looking out at me in the morning mirror? Strange, really, how after years of hacking and compromising the

5

old romantic seriousness remains. I still want to do something real. I'm still the boy I was, with my rented Bolex and my rainbow dreams, filming the streets of Brooklyn in an attempt to film my soul, believing that because I chose to point my camera at something, it somehow mirrored me. My stubborn integrity, my jejune ambitions. What to do with it? Film it, of course. But how?

My picture in *Time.* "Triumph in Cannes." "Burly, genial Stephen Mandreg, 33, is perhaps the most inventive and accessible of the new breed of American comic realists." And the damn thing is, my stupid heart was pounding as I read the thing. "Says Mandreg: 'Hollywood is first and foremost a kind of idea, and not necessarily a bad one.' " Professionalism is what I meant, technical skill and the best equipment, but they left out the qualifications. Mangled by *Time.* Genial indeed! But imagine my mother when she sees it. What, she'll say, you couldn't put on a tie?

The gun terrifies him because he can imagine himself using it. We are all capable of murder, we dream of it, but, of course, few of us do it. The fear that our thoughts and fantasies may become real. Relates to the anxiety of creation.

Supper in a restaurant down by the docks. A crammed self-conscious sort of place, candles, dried blowfish dangling from the ceiling, a star in Michelin. An old blotched mirror covered most of one wall, the kind they put in to provide an illusion of depth, magical space, a familiar trick akin to some of my own techniques. Ate squid in some kind of pink and piquant sauce, drank a wine called *blanc de blanc.* Eating alone is a furtive business, a kind of masturbation. I was spying on the place through the mirror, afraid of meeting eyes. At another table a Frenchman was entertaining his *enfants* with sleight-of-hand stunts involving spoons and corks and glasses, while his wife yawned and sim-

mered and occasionally glanced at me. There was a lady in blue
selling flowers, a blind man peddling lottery tickets. The waiter,
black-haired, red-shirted, looked vaguely deranged. A red flush
had spread across his forehead and he seemed to be gritting his
teeth. Some of this detail is extraneous, some crucial. Which is
which? Does it matter? Was my solitude the key? Outside on the
quay, someone, some American tourist, I suppose, some unknown
brother of mine, started to sing, rather boozily—

> Goodnight, Irene, goodnight, Irene
> I'll see you in my dreams—

and that random cojoining of the song, the place, the food, the
mirror, set off something in me.

How to describe it? It was one of those heightened moments
of transition, like an internal wind beginning to blow, a rear-
rangement of thought and mood as perceptible and permanent as
stepping through a door. I know, I know, it's just a drift of
adrenaline, a rush of blood to the brain. But it has stirred a
memory, a sharp, sensual memory, which may be all I need.

Let's get it down right. How old was I—ten, twelve, fourteen?
There in my pajamas at the window (must have been late at
night), stirred from my bed and perhaps from my sleep by the
sound of someone singing that same song, a Weavers hit, out
there on Montgomery Street. How he came through the schoolyard and down the schoolyard steps, taps on his heels, heels
clattering, singing loud enough to wake the whole neighborhood,
and hammering a few tom-tom beats on the metal of the candy
store's newspaper stand—good old Bono. Black pants, black
jacket, black curly hair, and a V of red, the only touch of color,
his shirt showing through in the lamppost light. Crossed Montgomery Street, passed beneath my window (never saw me, I'm
sure), vanished around the corner still singing. And I keep
remembering how, hiding there, my heart was stirred.

Bono. A movie about him? Bono selling syrupy shaved-ice

7

snowballs from a pushcart, Bono delivering groceries, Bono chasing Murphy out of the schoolyard, Bono smacking a tennis ball over the roof of 480 (and I later found it, sodden, in the puddle of a clogged drain, back there in that maze of alleys and courtyards).

Bono Bono Bono.

Bono on a Sunday morning in a Dodger cap, with a wad of chewing tobacco bulging his jaw, pounding his mitt, spitting brown juice, hollering, the quintessential shortstop. "Run, you goddam little Jewboy, run!" All the ambling and idle grace of perpetual, pointless youth—he just never grew up, that Bono.

The felt memory, behind the merely sensual ones, never so clear before, is how I longed to be him.

A period piece. A movie about the fifties, Brooklyn, schoolyards and candy stores, about the loss of innocence, about things ending and things falling apart, about being stuck and breaking free, Bono in the center of it. A movie about Montgomery Street, a lost world.

Bono finds a gun?

Sleep on it.

———

A movie about Bono and his sad, perpetual youth. He is thirtyish when we meet him, a kid at heart. Lives in the unpaved lane behind the synagogue, in that row of tar-papered houses across from the police station—a little Italian world behind the Jewish façade of Montgomery Street.

Black pants, red shirt. Thickly muscled, with a neck on him like a bull. The joy of him, the playfulness. His aversion to work.

Lives with or near old Dominic, blind and amputated, dying of diabetes, of the sweetness of life. Stuck in a wheelchair, eroded by age and illness. An era will die with him.

Make it clear that Bono is fated to end up like Dom, a life of odd jobs, a lingering miserable death. Suggestion of circles closing around him, a flux of energy circumscribed. Dom is Bono grown old and fat and sick and blind.

Who loves Bono? Who does Bono love?

He is self-contained, complete unto himself, a figure of solitude. Everyone knows him, admires him, but he has no real friends, no love, no family, no ties—except for Dom, who's like a Dorian Gray image of himself.

Everything stripped down to the bare processes of time and life and community. The synagogue and the police station.

Playing. Bats and balls. Phallicine. Bono used to be a grounds keeper at Ebbets Field, but they tore it down and built that big brick co-op. He believes O'Malley killed Brooklyn, took the life out of it, when he moved the Dodgers. He suffers the inevitable pain of change. Once he almost went professional but they wanted to send him to Moline, Ill., and he couldn't stomach the thought of going. He dreams of following the Bums to California. He just can't get them out of his blood. Memories. How he used to sit in the bleachers with his mitt, waiting to catch home runs. Trophies and banners on his walls. Dodger yearbooks, World Series souvenirs. Pictures of Billy Cox, the Duke, Pee Wee Reese. Wears that old Dodger cap with the big white B for Brooklyn on a royal-blue field.

"They murdered the place when they moved, just murdered it."

"He's all heart, that Bono."

A contrasting character who's all head.

Heart, earth.

They are digging up the sidewalk on Montgomery Street; jackhammers, violent noise, rich damp black earth showing through, a break in the gray artifice of pavement. It's experienced as a kind of threat.

The street itself as a kind of character; the importance of place.

But what's the story?

Bono with a gun. Or better: Dom has a gun and Bono takes it because he's afraid Dom will shoot himself, end his misery. The Catholic ban on suicide.

"I'm going to hell anyway."

Bono loses the gun and someone else finds it. A gun floating loose on Montgomery Street. A madman with a gun.

Too melodramatic.

Not if the gun doesn't go off.

Scene: a man with a gun is being faced down by the cops. Play off against the expectation of violence. Thwart them. The poor fellow never intended to use the gun but the mere sight of it sends people into hysterics. It's all a misunderstanding. In the end we are forced to live up to other people's expectations. We are what others make us. Trying just to be himself, wondering what he is.

He's Bono's antithesis.

A bald, dark, heavy-bearded fellow, always needing a shave. There's a pimple on his forehead, a boil, blazing red, about to burst. He can scarcely contain his rage. When we first see him he points an angry forefinger at someone (Bono? Bono's singing has disturbed his sleep?)—fires, pow, pow, pow, just like that.

The kids in the neighborhood run around playing gun games learned from movies. "You're dead, Billy the Kid, I shot you clean through!"

Killing Montgomery Street.

Jewish, married, stuck. Name? Abe, Isaac, Jake, Joe, Moe, Leo. Leo Feuer. A smoldering man, a conflagration in his veins. Fortyish, eyes bleary with suppressed fury. Fury and mire. Visual images of verbal puns. Make it fun to do, fun to see. Glum material infused with the pleasures of film-making.

His shrewish wife.

They were all more or less shrewish on Montgomery Street.

"Never marry a local girl."

There's been a fire in the neighborhood. We see the boarded-up ruins of—what?

Don't be too fancy. Rely on memory. Make it real.

All those textures of wood, charred brick, broken glass.

Film on location. More freedom if you keep the costs down. The feel of the place. The colors, the faces, the buildings. "Montgomery Street"

Dom: domed, doomed. The pleasure dome has become a death trap. The mustiness. His ailing wife shuffling around in old bedroom slippers. Her swollen legs sheathed in baggy stockings. No one to help out. The community is breaking down.

Events have to force Bono to accept change. Dom's death. Then he meets a girl. She's a threat to his freedom, but what does that freedom amount to?

It's all a bit of a cliché, isn't it? Jewish *kopf* envying the grace and vitality of the *goyische* body.

Don't go too fast. Play with it awhile. Let it simmer.

Strange how memory comes and goes, how ephemeral, how unreliable, how just plain messy it is. Why now, here, am I so stricken with Montgomery Street? This afternoon, on the beach, I fell into a kind of meditative half-doze, with the sun turning the inner screen of my eyelids red, and images of Brooklyn poured out of me. It was like watching a random assortment of rushes—though I suspect there's some hidden pattern to it. And I felt just that mingling of pleasure and anxiety (what next?) you feel watching a good movie.

So much of it is buried in me, is me, waiting to be exposed. More material than I know what to do with.

I could do Bono, spin a dream of him, but it's not really Bono I'm interested in, or rather not just Bono, but all that Bono implies. It's the street itself, my own boyhood, the submerged images of my own aspirations. The rhythms and cycles of the place. The way a locale impinges upon you, makes you a part of itself. How

11

you seek to escape it. Bono, in a sense, is free because he doesn't seek freedom. The rest of us became slaves to our desire to escape. Look at Georgie, look at me.

A movie about Brooklyn, about the way a place makes you what you are.

If I manage to do it, will anybody care?

———

Firecrackers in the schoolyard. A cherry bomb exploding in a garbage can, the lid flying up. The fat orange-haired lady who used to come down the block clutching the hand of her fat orange-haired androgynous son. Some moron learning to play bagpipes, the distant impossible skirl of that music on a Sunday morning. The red neon Breyer's sign buzzing and flickering in the candy store window. NO BALL PLAYING AGAINST THIS WALL!!! The woman in black who moved in with her cats, and how we all decided later that she and Kahn's sister were lesbians. The old woman who jumped off the roof, plunging like a bundle of rags through the agony of air, and the sickening thump of her body when she hit. Working for Korski: the gallons of Rose-X I shlepped up out of the basement, and delivering a case of toilet paper in that nonsensical baby buggy, and my fantasies about that old reb's wife. The janitors: drunken Willy and terrifying James—how we thought he caught squirrels and cooked them for dinner, and how scary the basements always were. Paisley shirts, riveted belts, combat boots. Yo-Yos. Johnny-on-the-Pony and ringalievio. "Free!" Hide-and-seek: looking for Barry and Barry had gone home. The Good Humor man. That power station on Nostrand Avenue, the hum of the dynamos, the dim mysterious gated interior, and always what seemed to be the same old grizzled Irishman sitting out front on a bentwood chair, priest guarding a temple. Whitey's fix-it shop. The children lurking behind the counter at the Chinese laundry. How they came to rip up the sidewalk on Yom Kippur. "Just imagine," my mother would say. A couple of goons loading furniture onto a Mayflower

moving van for the escape to Long Island. The blacks and the
Hasidim moving in. The way the *Hasidim* would go out walking
on the *shabbos* with their fur hats and their thin white hands
always clasped behind their backs. Their kids, with the *peyus*
tucked behind their ears, as ashamed of their traditions, their
past, as we were. Weekends. Hanging around. Transistor radios,
basement parties. Bensonhurst. Where's that? Bobby coming
home drunk that night, and poor Michelle, and how I thought I
was in love. Marvin, the mongoloid—that kid with cerebral palsy
(name?) and that crazy Italian kid with the canes and braces
always picking a fight. "Nellie put your belly next to mine!" The
men coming home from work with the inevitable newspaper
folded under an arm or stretching a jacket pocket. The fire alarm
on the corner: mustn't touch! So many taboos. So many noes. Cop
cars. That red-eared cop who pulled his gun and chased Van up
New York Avenue for selling firecrackers. What's a penny made
out of? What's a dirty penny made out of? Going to Coney
Island, Nathan's, a lovely binge. "Make a *himalacheh* in the old
man's back and somebody stuck his finger in." The *yentehs*
hanging out of windows. "Ruthie, come up, I make you eat!"
And all the old fogies sitting in a circle of folding chairs under a
lamppost, fanning themselves with handkerchiefs, and grumbling
about the *shvartzes* through the long and hot and lonely summer
night.

Amuse them. Make them laugh, make them cry. Even better
nowadays: shock them, frighten them silly. After all, they go to
the movies to learn how to feel. We are pedagogues of the
emotions. And I have to learn to accept it, or else go back to
16mm and being my own sound man.

Some choice.

"If you Endeavor to Please the Worst, you will never Please the
Best. To Please all is Impossible."

13

Time and transience. Things breaking down, things wearing thin, things being used up, eaten up, finished.

A way of life is coming to an end.

Leo is at the end of his savings; Dom is wasting away; the neighborhood is deteriorating, becoming a slum. But it's not the mere social process I'm interested in.

Bono pours the last drops of a Mission grape down his throat, squeezes the bottle, savors the final sweetness. A kid comes into the candy store and spends his final pennies—for what?

"Is there any food left in the house?"

"How much time is left?"

"Hey, you guys, it's getting too dark to play!"

Dom: "There's not much left of me."

The fabric on the sofa in Leo's apartment is worn to threads; the seat of his pants is shiny. Torn seats in the candy store, the woolgray stuffing showing though. Ripped Levi's. Toes popping out of old Keds. The school windows are broken.

Narrow it in time. Make it all take place in the summer of 1960, the end of an era, the end of one vision of America and the start of another. Eisenhower and his soothing era-to-era grin. Old soldiers never die, they just fade away. Like the Cheshire cat, another grin. The course of a summer. Giving way to fall. Vacations. Going to the Catskills. Kids bored, waiting for school to start again.

Change: process.

And against all this the things that are permanent: sky, sun, music, earth, Bono.

But what's his story?

With Dom. The gun. Takes it. Loses it. A girlfriend. Playing ball in the schoolyard with the kids. Pretty thin stuff.

The trouble is he's more an image than a character. He doesn't aspire, he doesn't act. Nothing can happen to him.

Then let him be the base against which everything else can be measured. He slides toward the periphery. We will catch only glimpses of him. He exists insofar as he affects others. Focus on what you know.

Who then occupies the crucial center?

Leo. Fortyish, unemployed. He lost his last job because he couldn't control his temper. A short, nasty, brutish sort of fellow, who lives with his wife and his kid in an apartment that reeks of potted meat.

"Hey, mister, get the ball please!" He ignores it, or kicks the ball into the gutter.

He quarrels with the neighbors. They whisper about him. His wife nags him. The boil on his forehead is about to explode. His kid is fourteen, on the verge of transformation. It's all beginning to overwhelm the guy. His kid's hatred. A fight.

He's afraid of time and change, afraid he'll plunge right through the mirrory surfaces of things, lose the world.

Then he finds the gun. It stirs up murderous impulses in him. His angry fantasies. His fear of violent madness. We see him sitting and fondling the thing. His impotence, his terror. Will he go berserk and kill someone? He—

———

Don't trust that glib flow of images, the rush of memory, the sirens of recollection. Bleak fantasies might provide a clue, but don't mistake them for reality. Why, now, this obsession with Montgomery Street, a place and a life I fled just as soon as I possibly could? Where is it leading me? My notes on Bono smack of condescension, and Leo is just a remnant of some old nightmare of mine.

I want to do Brooklyn in 1960, the street, the change. But I haven't yet found the characters I need. It's not broken and pointless lives I want to film. There would be no fun in it.

Dozens of characters, quick comic sketches hovering on the periphery, each of them potentially central but for the choices the mind behind the camera has made. Each of them has to be given a story, a scrap of life. Korski and his family. The candy store people. The neighborhood nice guy who comes home drunk. The woman who jumped off the roof. The world of the kids. Some old people, salt of the earth. A bookie. The Italians. The janitors. Things that happen just offscreen impinging on things that we see. What I want is not the usual rigmarole of a neat and selfcontained world. You have to learn to live with the mess, work in all the rich and impossible texture of life. A realism so real it becomes an artifice.

Organize it not around story, but around time and place. It all happens on a single day. A Friday. The week is ending, the summer is ending, the fifties are ending. The Friday before Labor Day in 1960. Nixon/Kennedy. Sputnik. Civil rights. The Congo.

Tell Mort to put a researcher on it.

That day a heat wave breaks in a tropical storm, rain scouring the streets, people hurrying to cover, everyone gets soaking wet, and then cooler air, a whiff of autumn, moving in.

A day in the life of Montgomery Street.

"The best American films, with few exceptions, are exquisitely accurate in recording the details of the outer world, and wholly spurious in portraying the felt tones of life." True?

Someone gets a new car. We see him in the morning polishing it, rubbing the last bit of shine in with his sleeve, preening it. He drives away. When he comes home, toward evening, a fender is bashed.

Late in the afternoon, a Good Humor truck, the ringing bells a counterpoint to several things all going on at once. Clocks. A church bell tolling the hours. Images of change, decay, life drifting slowly and awkwardly toward death. The desire for escape. Going up to the roof. Those lesbians. Airplanes, fireworks, stars. Wanting to fly.

"I'm flying. Oh God, oh God, I'm flying!"

Z on the phone: "Brooklyn? Brooklyn? Well, maybe, sure, why not? A period piece, kids with d.a.'s, tailfins, I like Ike, a little messing around. A nostalgia thing, the trade that goes to those rock 'n' roll revivals. Maybe. Write it up and we'll see."

A mind that thinks in billboards. At least he didn't say put a love story in.

Funny how it comes and goes, memory, inspiration, how unreliable it is.

Afternoon on the beach. The sun, the sand, the water, a big gray dog playing in the surf. You can't rush it, you have to let it come. I wish I could know that I was really onto something good, that this is the right material for me. But on the other hand my doubts seem mostly commercial. The game we have to play: how close can you come to seriousness and still sell the product? Can you make a living trying to please the best?

"Obscurity is neither the Source of the Sublime nor of anything Else."

Proud, stubborn Blake.

"To Generalize is to be an Idiot."

"Some Men Cannot see a Picture except in a Dark Corner."

Movie theaters he must have meant, the old gnome.

I'm feeling queasy. Too much sun, I guess.

A story about love. A first love, the most puppyish kind of love. A love that tries to live out in life those images of love that Hollywood spawns. Adolescent romanticism stubbing its nose against a flat hard world. Love that is ignorant of the real tumult of flesh, the mackerel-crowded seas. A boy coming of age on

17

Montgomery Street, discovering the dark commotion that lies beneath the gray surfaces of things. But do it lightly, a chance for parody.

He's Leo Feuer's kid. Having to grow up with an ignorant and angry father. How in the end you find yourself becoming the father you used to despise. But it has to be more than a piece about kids. He's just one element in the blend. Need someone who's come out the other end, a contrast, a link. Lots of mirrors. But not Leo. Someone with savvy, a kind of wisdom. How much leeway do I have? Make them laugh, and everything else will follow.

Name?

Stevie Feuer.

It was, after all, a popular name. There were at least three of us on Montgomery Street.

Stevie Feuer. Fourteen years old.

Plumpish, pink-faced, soft, unformed. He wears a cotton polo shirt, red and yellow striped. His legs are rubied with the clots of picked mosquito bites. (Insects: mosquitoes, flies, gnats, someone trapping a fly in a soda bottle, someone smashing a silverfish in a bathtub.)

There are soft people and hard people, the sick and the well. Stevie learning to be hard.

His hair is cut short and bristly on top, long and slicked back at the sides: a flat-top.

Those pubescent changes in size and shape and hairiness and hardness haven't yet happened to him. A late bloomer. What has gone wrong? Wonders if he is doomed to be perpetually fuzz-cheeked, soft, slow. When we first see him, early that morning, he's running in the schoolyard, trying to get in shape, trying to jar his body into that metabolic process he craves. Scene with his buddies in a locker room, the Boys Club. Those awful comparisons kids make. He cringes, hides. The idiotic and permanent shame of it.

As he runs he pretends he's flying. Able to leap tall buildings at a single bound. His mind has fed upon comic book heroes, Superman, Captain Marvel. *Shazam!* The subway tunnel where the ancients gave secret powers to Billy Batson, crippled newspaper boy. Scene: Stevie on the subway, riding in the first car, looking down the tunnel, the lights streaking past. You have to plumb the subterranean if you want to learn to fly.

Where's he going?

To Chinatown, to buy firecrackers. With a friend who's convinced him to go partners on a case of firecrackers to sell in the schoolyard. Montgomery Street entrepreneurs. Dreams of being old enough to drive, buy "wheels," escape the "rut."

Firecrackers in the schoolyard, the last big bang of summer.

He made his money working for Korski, delivering groceries in that ancient rattan baby cart. A plodding, unmanly sort of job. He has to struggle with an enormous carton of toilet paper. The goatish old Yid with the beautiful wife.

Bono delivers groceries on a swift, wholly masculine bike. Kids Stevie as he goes by. "I'm better than all of them." "I'll show them."

His epiphany on the train.

———

Letter from E. She's fine, the kids are fine, everything's fine, send money. The bitch. Saw my picture in *Time* and thinks I've become a millionaire.

———

Scenes: Stevie running in the schoolyard; having breakfast with his mother; drinking a soda in the candy store (the mirrored nook); working for Korski, delivering an order to Dom in that musty sad house. Stevie and the rabbi's wife. Stevie off to Chinatown with his pal. Stevie on the subway. Coming home, stuck, that thunderstorm. People beginning to panic. His epiphany. Returns to Montgomery Street soaking wet. Funny bits, caricatures. No one will see the symbols but the symbols will

19

amuse me. Like the hidden pattern of *Centerpiece;* they don't have to perceive it, but it's important that it's there. That's how you please Z and manage still to please yourself. Evening: his father comes home, a fight. No. He's broken the circle of his boyhood, he's beyond that now. Then in the schoolyard, selling firecrackers. The cops arrive. Chased by a cop with a gun, hides in the maze of alleys behind the façade of Montgomery Street. Another world. Physical manifestations of mental states. Bricks and windows are reflections of dreams. Peeking in windows, eavesdropping, like going to a movie. What does he see? Later, returns to the schoolyard, a local freak performing "Nellie put your belly next to mine." Nightmarish, crude. His reaction. Later with the girl whose father comes home drunk. Call her Anita. She's a big, breasty girl with a poor complexion. He tries to comfort her. It's mostly sympathy which he confuses with love. The way it started with E. But also his needs. They kiss good night. So now he's got a girlfriend, has re-entered the circle. Home. The street closing around him. Goes to bed. No climax, no big ending. But connect it all to another character or characters. A surface both simple and clear. Being what other people expect you to be versus being yourself, whatever that is. A boy grows up, a man grows old, a neighborhood decays, the world moves a day closer to the end of time. Bleak, really, but for the gorgeous clutter of life.

Dawn. From high above we see the sprawl of Brooklyn in grainy and monotonous twilight. Zoom slowly in on Montgomery Street as the titles begin. Gray buildings. A pattern of lit windows. Streetlamps blinking off. A boisterous newspaper truck tosses out bales of newspaper, which tumble and settle on the sidewalk near the candy store. We glimpse a cat at play among garbage cans. The head of Bertie Grossman, goiter and all, materializes in a window, vanishes again. Korski down below is hauling crates of milk into his shop. Make him a roly-poly man in a gray smock, bent round like a reaper in a Breughel. The scrape of the milk crates on the sidewalk. We also see an old Italian handyman, a friend of Dom's, off early to work: grizzled, waddling, chewing, grumbling to himself, pushing a lawn mower along the pavement. Bagpipe music starts to come from somewhere. Cut to: a teen-age mongoloid named Jeremy. Huge-eared, shambling. He clutches a stick in one hand and something small, a coin, in the other. He goes to the candy store and presses his nose flat against the window. Not open yet, how sad. He raps on the glass. Then he plants his coin in his pocket, clambers up the schoolyard steps, starts pounding his stick on the iron gate. The chukchukchuk of it resounds over the street. A car goes by, whispering tires. A church bell begins to toll seven, like a new theme in a *symphonie concrète*, as we cut to: the big glassed front door of an apartment building. It yawns open, mirroring stores, cars, Korski, fire escapes in its rotating glass, and Stevie Feuer emerges running. He runs out of the shop to his left and the slow door, mirroring everything again, but now in reverse, clamps shut shuddering against its iron frame.

(Introduce some other character here?)

Stevie running in the schoolyard. At first he's imagining he's Captain Marvel, arms out, flying, an invisible red cape billowing behind him, the wind whistling through his hair. But after a lap or two, he's wheezing and spent, entropic. That scene in *On the Waterfront* when Brando, beaten and bloodied, has to make it up the ramp and into the warehouse so the dockmen will follow him back to work, break John Friendly's power. Parody that here. Instead of Eva Marie Saint and her beautiful eyes, the spectator is the mongoloid. The world blurring in front of Stevie; the schoolyard through a distorting lens. Get there, get there. Face fiery red, he makes it to the steps, wheezing.

Main titles end.

Jeremy: Wanna play?

(From play to games to work, the grim process of growing up.)

Stevie: Hell, no.

J: I have my own ball—look!

He produces from his pocket a shiny old Spalding, no doubt dead, and holds it with awkward fingers in front of his face.

S: Later, Jeremy. Okay?

More of this.

Jeremy begins to turn the ball round and round, looking at it. Eventually he seems to get lost in looking at it, as though his whole world has shrunk itself into the ball: his idiot's inward fascination.

A bit of mess dribbles from his nose.

S: Hey, Jeremy, for chrissake, wipe your nose, will ya? Come on now, Jeremy, wipe your nose.

J:———

S: Hey, come on, you have a hanky, don't you? Use your hanky, Jeremy.

Still no response. Jeremy is humming softly to himself. Stevie reaches for but then can't quite bring himself to touch the mongoloid's arm, that mottled skin.

Move in tight on the ball going round and round. Cut to the yolk of a fried egg, Stevie's breakfast. His mother.

Lots and lots of circles.

———

Stevie runs into Korski.

S: Good morning.

K (abruptly): See you sharp at ten.

———

Sometime during the day we catch a glimpse of a cat lying squashed in the gutter. The smell starts affecting everyone.

———

We cut from X back to Stevie, who is sitting in the double-mirrored nook at the back of the candy store; he's washing down his breakfast with a Mission grape and reading a book or magazine. He looks up and sees himself reflected and re-reflected and re-reflected again, a multitude of Stevies, all pink-faced and damp, duplicated to infinity. All of these Stevies rather sheepishly grin. He returns to the book. What's he reading? A Captain Marvel comic.

No.

Make it *The Theory and Practice of Hell.* The concentration camps. Those familiar nightmare images of boxcars, camp gates, bunk beds crammed with skeletal survivors, piles of hair, gold teeth, glass eyes. The scarred victims of medical experiments, the shower rooms, the ovens. Mountains of corpses, bulldozed into a pit. And he's not so much reading as devouring the grim gray sandwich of photographs bound into the book's center.

His reaction: it excites him, fascinates him, as well as disturbs him. He licks his lips, arches tense shoulders. Dachau, Buchenwald, Auschwitz: we can sense the names tolling in his head. The camps are implicit in Montgomery Street.

How?

The atmosphere of the place, the sense of boundaries, the edginess, the relentless security, the mute anxiety, the craziness around the edges, the maddening grayness . . . how much of it was some sort of secret response to the camps? Or to what the camps were an emblem of.

Remember how if some poor shmuck of a bus driver happened to be surly, my mother would mutter "anti-Semit." Believing that in the soul of every Gentile lurked the Nazi beast.

Do I really need to go into this?

What was it? Horror? Dread? Anger? Guilt? The fascination of the abomination? Or just a sense of relief, a hidden macabre smile at one's own incredibly good luck?

God bless America.

The quiet hostility between the refugees and the American-born Jews. Our sense of Hitler's mark on them.

Korski was in the camps. He has a number on his arm, and he always wears long sleeves, even in hot weather. Because, and this is incredible, the tattoo shamed him. Why?

We see him as a bland, roly-poly, rather mean-hearted little man, with a fat wife, also a refugee, and a couple of nasty, scrabbly kids with shaved heads and dirty hands and *peyus* tucked behind their ears. (We can catch a glimpse of them playing in front of the store, some mean little game.) It troubles Stevie that a man who lived through all that horror and holocaust can now be so rosy and smirking, bossing him around, making bad jokes, smelling of sweat and greed and kosher soap. How does someone manage to look into the foul rag-and-bone heart of things and not be somehow either sanctified or annihilated? Why didn't heaven open up, the sky pour down its wrath and vengeance on Auschwitz? Stevie had expected Korski to give off some special air or light.

It's not just evil that's banal; survival is, too.

Some other, older character will have to articulate some of this. But, implicitly, it's on Stevie's mind.

How to suggest the substreams that flow beneath the ordinary dull surface of Montgomery Street?

A character capable of insight and articulation. Don't limit yourself to the childish and dumb. Don't cut yourself off completely from those oh-so-articulate charmers of *Centerpiece*. But also don't be glib.

The pathos of intelligence operating in a minatory and limited world. In the grayness a glimmer of rainbow dreams.

But what would such a person be doing there?

Might as well ask if I really want to do this at all, confine myself for the next year to a single day on Montgomery Street.

———

In a sense, all times and places exist in any single time and place. Perhaps each of the characters can suggest a different historical

24

moment, a different culture, not literally perhaps, but at least as a source of detail; their idiosyncrasies, their beliefs. Touch the world at any point and the whole trembles.

―――――

The notion that Brooklyn somehow wasn't real, wasn't where life was authentically lived, thus couldn't be fit material. A fallacy.

―――――

Rely on rich texture, the sights, the sounds, the smells of the place. The way the sidewalk in front of the candy store was stained black by bits of melted wax from those little penny bottles of sugar water. Wildlife: sparrows, cats, the occasional squirrel, a bright butterfly dancing above the grimy thick leaves of the bushes behind an iron fence. The clinging heat of a summer day. Coming home from the beach, that sandy feeling, the way your throat would ache when you took a deep breath. The way tough guys rolled a pack of cigarettes in the sleeve of a T-shirt. Bell-bottoms. Pinkus jumping from the fire escape when his parents made him stay in his room. The time he told me how women bleed. Ruthie with her pants down under the steps. Stoopball, pitching pennies. Dogshit. The oily rainbow slick on top of a puddle. Breadcrusts lying in the gutter. The mess of a dropped ice cream stick. A lost dented hubcap. "Ashes, ashes, we all fall down." What I don't remember I can always invent. I just love it, that rush of vision, when it begins to come. Nothing like it, nothing quite the same. Heels and baseball cards. A man who wears both belt and suspenders. What fun!

―――――

The candy store. Bertie Grossman is a fat lady with a goiter. She keeps the goiter masked behind a dingy white man's handkerchief tied around her neck. Sometimes the handkerchief slips. She is thick and fleshy, her joints babyishly hidden beneath rolls of fat. Rather simple. *"Oy, veh ist mir!"* Let the minor characters be stereotypes who eventually transcend themselves.

The husband, Willy. He's all spiky gray hair and stubble and tragic eyes. The kids in the neighborhood call him Crazy Willy. He's addicted to gambling. He sends Stevie to the newsstand near the subway to buy "the green National."

"You tell him to put it in a paper bag. He'll know."

The sad absurdity of trying to keep a secret that everyone knows. Gossipy Montgomery Street.

Willy is sitting in the booth behind Stevie drinking a cup of coffee. It might be, judging from his expression, a cup of bile. Maybe let his image join Stevie's in the labyrinth of mirrors.

Later on in the day someone comes into the candy store and catches Willy reading the tip sheet. He crumples it up, trying to hide it. Still later Willy is seen on the phone. He's lost. We can read it in his face. All of which must be almost subliminal, mere background for some other action.

We're still in Stevie's POV.

A customer comes in.

Bertie: So look who's back in town! So how was the cruise?

Cust: It was gorgeous, what can I say, simply gorgeous! And the food!

B: I wish I could go myself.

Willy grumbles.

B: Mister Bigshot over there!

Willy curses her. They begin a brawl. The customer flees. We are focused on Stevie, bemused.

Etc.

———

Lester. A tall thin ambling boy with a recessive chin and an Adam's apple bobbing in his long neck, a kind of Abbott to Stevie's plump Costello. He's a real conniver, a kid you just know will go far. He peddles firecrackers; later on, when he gets to college, he'll sell term papers, maybe drugs. Then I suppose he'll go into the entertainment business, finish up in Gucci boots and pink suits, smoking cigars, with hair in his ears. Oh, Lester, how well I've come to know you!

He oozes into the candy store, sees Bertie is distracted, slips a Baby Ruth into his pocket. Goes to the table, grabs Stevie's soda, gulps it down, Adam's apple bobbing—Stevie's own sweet Mission grape. Hapless Stevie can only watch. "Ah! Thanks." Rubs his tummy, belches.

S: Hey, you know you can ask.

L: Whacha reading?

He takes the book, leafs through it, throws it down. Those horrific images mean nothing to him; they merely justify his cynicism.

I suppose there had to be more to him than that, but never mind.

All long legs, he slides into the booth opposite Stevie.

Kids' street talk, oddly precocious.

L (suddenly serious): Listen, will you lend me ten bucks?

S: Go to hell.

L: Listen. Give me a tenner and, I promise, you'll get back twelve tonight.

S: Where am I supposed to get ten bucks?

L: Hey, come on, man, you got to help me out.

Ruefully, dimly, Stevie admires Lester, craves his friendship, envies his show of worldliness, his moxie.

S: What for?

L: I'm going to Chinatown to get some stuff. I need some capital. Last big bang of summer, man—understand?

Lester is always in motion, fidgeting, toying with things, a victim of energy that is primarily spiritual seeking a vent in a wholly material world. With the wet bottom of that soda bottle he makes a pattern of intersecting circles on the red Formica, a three-ring sign. Ask the man for Ballantine. The Dodgers have gone west and in 1960, in Brooklyn, you have only the unlovable Yanks to root for. ("What's the score?" "Aah, they slaughtered 'em.")

L: Look, are we friends? I mean, wouldn't I do something for

27

you? Who tipped you off about Ruthie, huh? So I'm asking as a friend.

S: I don't have that kind of money.

L: Then how much you got? Seven? Five? You got five bucks?

S: Right now I'm broke.

L (voice rising): So you're really gonna be that way, huh? I mean, that's how you're gonna be.

S: If I had the money, I'd lend it to you, but I don't have it.

L: You get paid today, don't you?

How do the Lesters of the world manage to know everything? What are their sources? Stevie half suspects that Lester can read minds. The point is that while Stevie lives half in his own head, and so is constantly vague about things, Lester lives completely in the details of the world.

S (trying not to yield): I need that money for—

L: You'll have it. I said I'll pay you back tonight. Okay, I'll tell you what. We go partners on the deal. Sixty-forty, which is fair enough. Put up a tenner and you'll get back at least twenty.

S: When?

L: Tonight, man. We can't miss. Everybody's gonna be there. Last big bang of summer.

S: Okay, but I'm not just giving you the money. I'm going to Chinatown with you.

L: You sure you want to?

S: Why shouldn't I?

L (mockingly): No reason.

S: I'm not scared.

L: I didn't say you should be.

Finally they agree to leave at noon, when Stevie's finished work.

———

Z on the phone: "I've got a *femme* for you." They're off to Paris together and he wants me to come up to meet her. Says she's

Brooklyn to the core, so should be perfect for the picture. "You're still working on Brooklyn, right?" Seems he's practically promised her a role; says I won't be disappointed. Checked with Mort. Mort says she's a real thing and not just Z's latest bedmate. Called Z back. In the throes of creativity, I told him. Can't leave now. Sète's my inspiration. Let her come here to meet me. And just where the hell is Sète? he wanted to know. We left it at maybe.

Anyway, he seems to have sold himself the notion of a Brooklyn movie, and that's half the battle won.

Woke up in one of those moods this morning, had to struggle out of bed. I seemed to have spent the night dreaming of people mocking me. Things won't ever be as bad again as they were last year, but every so often there comes an echo of it, that same hot sense of unreality, and I find myself fighting to stay calm. It's nothing, of course, nothing, just the kind of thing you have to expect to go through after a divorce. You have to learn to feel yourself again. A blinking of the mind akin to the blinking of your eyes when you come out of a movie on a sunny afternoon. Or that moment of disorientation that comes as you slip into or out of a dream.

Stevie has spent the summer working for Korski, two hours a day, five days a week. Korski's customers are all refugees; the American-born of Montgomery Street do their shopping in Waldbaum's on Nostrand Avenue. That's where Bono works. Stratification. The refugees can trust Korski to keep kosher. The assimilated Jewish supermarket managers hire the *goyim* and the blacks to do the drudge work; Korski hires Stevie.

He gets seventy-five cents an hour plus tips, which don't amount to much. Have him complain to someone that the refugees are cheapskates. Two wholly separate Jewish worlds for Stevie to explore. His mother refers to the refugees as "real kikes." They no doubt thought of us as just more *goyim*. Or worse, I suppose. For the death camp survivors, we must have seemed degraded, obscene. Have to suggest somehow, without falling into cliché, the whole weird ethnic pecking order of a neighborhood that's in transition. The way it organizes itself around fear, dislike, grudging respect. That mulatto doctor around the corner; his neighbor, the Irish garbageman, moving out. That sense of community breaking down, which is the heart of the thing.

Stevie delivering groceries: montage. The geography, the nuances of landscape, the sheer physicality of the place. The police station and the synagogue facing each other across New York Avenue. The alleys lined with old garages, too small for new cars. The lane where Dom lives. The Italian poolroom. The big old private houses up along Crown Street, where the refugees lived, every other basement a *shul*. Where did their money come from? Go a couple of blocks farther north and black faces appear. Window shades instead of curtains, broken bottles, bits of glass, emblems of an advancing slum.

He meets Anita; the baby buggy embarrasses him.

Bono goes by on his bike.

A child is drawing an elaborate picture with pastel chalks on the sidewalk.

The shock of those *Hasidic* houses. Bearded little men come to the door with their fringes dangling, dig into deep pockets for a dime. The pink and scrubbed and nunlike women with scarves on their heads. The little children in gabardine, all big eyes, staring at Stevie as though he were a minor devil—and for them, of course, he is. He is beyond what they take to be the Law. He lives in a Torah-less world of forbidden foods, impossible anarchy.

Maybe towards evening Stevie should catch a glimpse of the *Hasidim* celebrating the *shabbos*. In a hot and airless room, with pale-blue walls and candles, the men are dancing in a circle while the women serve up plates of yellow cookies and glasses of kosher wine. A glimpse of the ecstatic brand of *Hasidim*, God-intoxicated, joined in an otherworldly and yet wholly sensual joy, something Stevie can never know. He stares in the window, sees a youngish *yeshiva bucher*, red-haired, pimply, with a wisp of beard and big blue fanatical eyes, clapping hands, dancing in the circle, going round and round. How can you tell the dancer from the dance? There is noise, sweat, uproar, a moment of joy. Community is there. Then someone, a big moon-faced woman, chases Stevie away from the window. Guilty, furtive, envious, hating, he plunges back to Montgomery Street, goes to the schoolyard. There he finds his friends and one of the local freaks. They are urging the boy to perform his "show." "Nellie put your belly next to mine." Another dance in a circle, community again, juxtapostition. Stevie's reaction. Fine.

A female lead? The rabbi's wife?

Stevie delivering a huge carton of toilet paper, pushing it in the baby buggy, struggling with it up a flight of stairs. Echo Laurel and Hardy delivering a piano.

The grocery store. A dingy place. Mrs. Korski, fat, red-cheeked, is behind the counter spreading a thick slab of butter on a Kaiser roll. She never intends to go hungry again. Korski, smocked, is piling cans and packages into a carton, preparing an order. He glances at the big round clock on the wall: three minutes after ten. Stevie has changed clothes: Levi's, a riveted belt. He looks older now, slightly comic, trying to look tough.

No greeting is exchanged.

K (all business): So. First you bring up a case toilet paper and deliver it, 404 Crown.

As far as they're concerned, he's beyond the pale.

When a customer comes in, Korski's manner changes completely, becomes polite, friendly, bantering in Yiddish.

Needs work.

I keep enjoying this place more and more. I like the market, the cheeses, the *charcuterie,* seeing the women go from stall to stall, gabbling with the merchants. This evening I went down to the quay to watch the fishing boats come in. Then I watched the old men play *boules* in the square. They seem to have been at it forever, that slow and careful game, and I love the way the small muscles of wrist and forearm respond to the practice of years. Technical skill. Self-assurance. They rue a bad shot, but accept a good one as expected. Then there's the sun, the beach, the water, the wine. I'm tan and fit and working well. There's community here, and though I remain merely an observer, I'm noticed now, my face has become familiar, and so the warm circle of it has come to include me. Which is what I've been after, isn't it? Odd, really, how I'm managing to feel at home.

It's partially the season, of course. August, vacation time. I suppose after Labor Day my inner clock will buzz and New York will beckon me.

How within the limits I've imposed do I delineate Stevie's fantasies about the rabbi's wife? Worse. How do I suggest *her* fantasies and still keep her subsidiary, avoid her point of view? To project fantasies literally on the screen is nonsensical. I hate the rippling dissolve, the interior world (which is felt) trans- formed into exterior objective images. Even Kurosawa himself couldn't do it successfully in *Dodes'ka-den.* Film is convincing only when it shows external reality. The inner life must be wholly implied. Have him talk about it to Lester? No, he wouldn't, and besides, that's a mere playwright's trick.

Moreover. How to suggest the netlike pattern of influences which underlie his life? Leah dominates his thoughts all morning, but she is practically absent from his world. His father may appear for only a scene or two, and that near the end, yet his presence is everywhere Stevie goes, that stolid, angry, limited man. As in life, these people must be seen as ultimately mysterious because they are compacted of other people we will never meet, actions and interactions we will never see. How do you film an invisible web?

Back up a bit.

Leah is young, pretty. Black hair, pink and white complexion, a sort of ingénue. As though she were the heroine of a Victorian novel, her pink bosom heaves. Her husband is an old man with a goatish gray beard, red-rimmed eyes, drab clothes, greedy lips, a medieval mind. All of history was there on Montgomery Street, all you had to do was look for it. It is a marriage by contract. Her feelings? We don't really have to know. But her smile is so innocent and pure and hungry it's an invitation to love. She is naïveté on the verge of depravity, a pink flower blossoming on the rim of the voluptuous abyss. Or so Stevie perceives her.

Depend upon the camera, caress her with it, let her play to it, make the audience tumesce for her.

Stevie's yearning is wild, extravagant, nonsensical. He has abused himself with her image. Am I getting too mawkish? Strange how that old pubescent excitement lingers in me still. Is that why I want to film this thing? To evoke her image again, do now what I couldn't do then? Stevie fancies himself a kind of cavalier: the lovely young ward stolen from her old and ugly and lustful guardian. All summer long he has been obsessed with a fantasy, the promise of a magical day to come when he will put down the grocery order and turn to find her reaching for him. A touch, a long-imagined moment of warmth, he believes, and he will be changed, changed utterly, becoming at last that hard bold image of a man he harbors. A jagged stick of lightning. *Shazam!* Which is, I suppose, where his fancy stops. The rest would be for him a red, hot and confusing blur. Fourteen, after all, is such an awkward age.

Don't forget: her allure is heightened in his mind by her connection to the camps. Does he imagine himself as liberator or Nazi beast? A little of both. And the old man becomes for him both his tormentor and his victim. All of which haunts him; none of which he actually sees.

———

Cut from X to Stevie in the grocery store cellar. Musty, gray. Cases of food, detergent, bleach, etc., piled up. Bugs. Spider webs. The possibility of mice. Bright red of Brillo boxes, adumbrations of pop art. A shaft of sunshine coming through the doorway, mote-infested light. He grabs a case of something, carrots, and starts up the steps, and there she is. His point of view from down below looking up at her into the dazzling brightness; she looks down at him and smiles. From that perspective she seems huge.

There's no sound at all.

He enters the store; she's there at the counter giving an order to Korski

He gawks at her.

As though from a great distance we hear Korski saying: "If the boy doesn't get around to it this morning, I'll bring it myself this afternoon."

The camera caressing her, Stevie's eyes: that will be enough.

Then Stevie having to rush through all the other jobs Korski gives him; keep the tension up. The clock. It's ten to twelve.

Finally: "Now you take this to—"

What has she ordered? That toilet paper. Oh, Leah, Leah, Leah shits!

Wheeling that toilet paper in the buggy; the poignancy of it; going up and down a curb.

Establish the husband. He comes down the stoop as Stevie arrives. "Ah, yes, from the grocer. You go up here. My wife she lets you in."

Struggling with the toilet paper up the steps, sweating, red in the face. The door opens on a long corridor; in the dim dusky interior, all strange smells and old books, she glimmers for him. She tries to help; awkwardly he tries to squeeze past her; there is a moment of scalding contact.

A glimpse of a bedroom, a bed. A small child stares up at Stevie.

A kitchen.

"You just put it here, please."

The lilt of accent in her speech. That smile. She's been cleaning house for the *shabbos;* a question mark of hair curls below her kerchief; her face is flushed. She sweeps the lock of hair away with the back of her hand and we glimpse her soft white underarm. Enchanting. The camera must practically kiss her there.

"So hot out, yes?"

Stevie's POV: her face, her neck, her breasts, her waist.

"Yes."

Her waist, her breasts, her neck, her face.

"Will you take some cold water?"

A moment of paralysis.

"No, thank you, I—"

Can't quite see it; how shall it go?

Let him be bolder than me.

She has her back to a window; again that radiance of light, the camera moving around it.

S (mumbling): You're very—

L: What?

S: You're—

Then heroically: I think you're very beautiful.

Her response shrivels him; she laughs, embarrassed for a moment, catches hold of herself and decides to respond as though to a child.

"Very nice of you to say it."

Maybe she even pats him on the head.

She fumbles in her apron, puts a coin into his hand.

And here's something for you.

The camera has now come around behind her; she makes a movement toward the door; in a long dolly shot we follow Stevie back through the long corridor, past the bed, the child, the door, down the steps into the blaze of the street, the waiting baby buggy. He kicks the thing and it tumbles over.

Another angle: tight on his hand. He opens a fist and we see one thin dime.

Idiot.

Cut.

He has lunch in Freedman's delicatessen on Nostrand Avenue. Two hot dogs with ketchup, fries, a Coke. Linger a moment on all those dangling salamis, the platters of potato salad and cole slaw, the vat of pickles, the knishes, the black-bow-tied waiter who seems to have come right off the Yiddish stage. There are cans of Heinz baked beans stacked in pyramids on a shelf in front of a mirror. Mr. Freedman himself. He opens a steamer and reaches in with a huge fork and plucks out of the delectable mist a pink corned beef. Suggest that Stevie's fondest memories will turn out to be gastronomical. The waiter and a customer are telling each other dirty jokes with Yiddish punch lines. Stevie listens, taking it all in. Need some action, some focus here, but it's the kind of thing you can work up on location. Don't close yourself off too much; leave space for the aleatory, some actor's bright idea.

Stevie and Lester ride the subway to Chinatown. They stand at the front window of the first car watching the blue telephone lights streak by. Remember how the bright rails, through a visual illusion, seem to be racing along with the train? Stevie is in love with subways. He loves it when an express train passes local stations, the blur of pillars and posters and light, and that marvelous sense that some physical law (Thou shalt stop!) has somehow been suspended just for him. They catch up to a local between stations, and for a moment they are in a race, neck and neck, until the local seems to slip backward and is lost at a station behind—the way friends and family slip away. Red lights up ahead turning green as you approach them. The motorman in his compartment, probably want a big black man, slightly bored, wearing grimy thick gloves, his hand clutching the dead-man's brake. Dust and bits of paper stirred by the wind whirl through the car. The blackness of the tunnel walls: how did they ever manage to get so dirty? The magic of it, riding to Manhattan, that bigger and somehow (it seemed) realer world. I still know the stations by heart: President Street, Franklin Avenue, Brooklyn Museum, Grand Army Plaza, Bergen Street, Atlantic Avenue, Nevins Street, Clark Street, where you got off to go swimming at the St. George Hotel, and then the long narrow half-cylinder of the deep cool tunnel under the East River. God, how many years has it been since I rode a subway to Brooklyn? Stevie, under the river, looking for leaks, a bit of water dripping down, first sign of collapse. How he would love to have a reason to pull the emergency cord! The train screeching to a stop, sparks flying, a flat spot ground into the circles of the wheels. He and Lester discuss it. They talk about jumping off the train and exploring the intricate maze of the subway system on foot. How dangerous would it be? What would you find down there? Rats, says Lester. Rats big as cats. Can you survive on your own? Sure. You could eat candy bars and peanuts bought in coin machines. Just don't step on the third rail. If a train was coming at you, you could squeeze against a wall, or even lie in the space between the tracks. Maybe Lester, long and lean, could; plump Stevie probably could not.

"I heard about a guy who did it."

"Yeah, sure."

They recall that it was in a deserted subway tunnel that Billy Batson met the ancients who taught him the magic word. Transfiguration is the essence of all adolescent, why not say all human desire. To be struck by lightning, to become Captain Marvel, to soar into the blue sky far above gray Montgomery Street with your red cape billowing behind you: this is what Stevie thinks he wants. And you can only learn the secret of metamorphosis in the dark, grimy, secret depths. What ever happened to Captain Marvel anyway, Lester wants to know. This is the sort of information Stevie has. Superman put him out of business, sued him for infringement of copyright. Somehow Captain Marvel was better, says Stevie. *Shazam!* What's in a word?

Canal Street.

"We get off here."

"Holy Moley!"

A wino at the subway entrance, red-eyed, filthy, a bottle in a paper bag.

———

Titles:

Montgomery Street
The End of Summer
9/2/60
The Block
Day Becomes Night

———

Chinatown, a visual feast. Wonder why it hasn't been used more often? Ideograms. Crowds. Telephone booths like small pagodas. Old Chinese men in those gray suits and loose shirts and bedroom slippers. Theaters playing movies you've never heard of. Do those doorways opening onto bleak hallways lead to opium dens? Restaurant windows, vats of boiling soup, strange pastries, dead ducks. Ivory gimcracks. Tourist buses. We glimpse Lester and Stevie through the crowd. They're smoking cigarettes, almost naturally. Red-eared cops from the precinct around the corner. Dragons. Remember the tong wars? Dress up someone like Charlie Chan, but you'll have to look quick to spot him. ("Maybe over the weekend we'll go eat chinks," Stevie's father will say.) Pell Street. Mott Street. Plug for King Wu. Stevie has been to Chinatown only once before; when he was a child his parents took him to see the Chinese New Year. He remembers the crowds, the din of the firecrackers, the gongs, the confusion, the huge red paper dragon slithering and dancing through the claustrophobic street. It had terrified him, they had to take him home. Now he is self-conscious. He rubs a sweaty palm on his jeans. He drags on his cigarette, starts to cough. Lester pounds his back. His eyes water. People are looking at him, or so he thinks. Sees a cop. Firecrackers are illegal. His impulse is to run.

L: What's the matter, you nervous?

S: No.

He looks up. The weather is changing, dark storm clouds moving in, swallowing the blue.

I can't recall anyone who has satisfactorily filmed a city sky—how the buildings limit it, how fragmented it is.

L: Okay, you wait for me here.

S (belligerent because scared): What do you mean, I wait for you here?

L: Just what I said. I have to go in alone.

S: The hell with that. I'm coming with you.

L: You can't, jerko. They won't sell if you're there.

S: Why not?

L: They don't know you. You think they sell to just anyone?

S (bitterly): You're full of it, Lester. You know that. You're really full of it.

L (patiently): What's all the fuss? Just wait here awhile.

S; How long you going to be?

L: A couple of minutes. Stop being such a baby.

S: I'm just trying to protect my investment, that's all.

L: Yeah, right. Don't worry about it.

S; Just hurry back, that's all.

Lester goes a step or two, comes back.

L: The money. Where is it?

S: Oh.

He leans against a wall, looks around, takes off his shoes, reaches in, pulls out a neatly folded ten-dollar bill. Slips it to Lester. Lester is amused.

L: Don't get into trouble while I'm gone. This is a tough neighborhood.

S; Very funny.

L (mocking): I'm just looking out for your welfare.

S: Go tell it to your old lady.

L: At least I got one.

S: With that moustache on her, I thought it was your father.

Lester smirks at the feeble retort, goes.

Long shot: Stevie waiting while the crowds of Chinatown swirl around him. He looks small and lost and far from home. Throws the cigarette away, as though there's no point smoking it now that Lester's gone. Chews his lip.

Two young toughs walk past him. They're maybe sixteen years old. Stevie tries to look nonchalant—tries so hard not to attract their attention that they can't help noticing him.

They walk a step or two past him, glance at each other, smile, nod, turn back.

Shoot the whole scene through a long lens; we catch only glimpses of it; people keep getting in the way. Other sounds on the sound track, voices drifting in and out.

Stevie seeks an escape. Dash into that restaurant? Too late. He tries to muster his courage, turns to face them.

Tone here is crucial. His fear is real but the danger is slight. A comic tension must be there.

The tough kids parody the leering bantering villainy of B

movies. Or Max and Al in "The Killers."

One's Italian, the other's black: the two bogeys of Jewish Montgomery Street. The Italian, Sal, has a pack of Camels rolled up in the sleeve of his aqua T-shirt. The black, Roy, wears a black kerchief over his "do." Stevie sees them as big and mean and ugly; we can see that they're also just kids.

Sal (to Roy): Here's a guy who's gonna help you out. (To S) My buddy here needs carfare to get home.

S (big, sick grin): Really?

Sal: Can you lend him a quarter? You must have a quarter you can spare.

A first faint rumble of thunder.

S: Really, I'd like to help you out, but I'm broke.

Sal: Hey, I only asked for a quarter.

S: Well, I'm meeting my pals here in a minute. One of the six of them might be able to—

But Roy has slapped Stevie's right-hand pocket; the clank of coins is heart-stopping.

Sal: You must have forgot about that money, kid.

Roy (a bit thick): Yeah, Sal, he must've forgot.

Sal: What about it, asshole?

S: But that's not my money. That's—

Roy (putting a hand on Stevie's arm): You think maybe he wants to walk around the corner with us, Sal?

Sal: What about it, asshole? Wanna walk around the corner?

S opens his mouth, can't speak, shakes his head.

Sal: Let's have a look at the money.

S: I guess I could lend you a quarter.

Fumbles in his pocket, produces a quarter.

Sal: Now the rest of it.

He pulls out more coins, hands them over. Roy pats the empty pocket.

Sal (smiling): That's being friendly, see. Remember it's just a loan. You come see us on Mulberry Street and we pay you back.

Roy (sneering): Yeah, asshole, you come up and see us.

They move away.

S (muttering): Shazam.

Thunder, a weak flash of lightning.

They come back at him.

Tight on Roy's mean face. Viciously: You say something?

S: I didn't say anything.

Sal (amused): Careful, kid, my friend has a bad temper. He may decide to cut you.

Roy: This boy called my mother a bad name. I heard him. Now I'm going to have to cut him.

S (terrified): I swear to you, I didn't say anything.

Roy: What'd you say about my mother?

Stevie's eyes. Cut in: Roy has taken a gravity knife out of his pocket, flicks it open, holds it with his fingers along the blade so Stevie can see it but people passing by can't. Stevie's eyes. The knife. Medium shot of the three of them.

S: Hey, look, I—

Roy's mock anger seems on the verge of becoming real.

R: He's trying to be a big man, Sal. I think I better cut him.

Sal: What about it, asshole? You a big man?

A miserable heartbeat.

S: No.

Sal smiles. Soothing: Maybe you got him wrong, Roy. He doesn't think he's a big man. (Throws a heavy arm around S's neck, breathes into his face.) You're a good kid, aren't you? You're just a good little asshole, right?

S:———

Sal (tightening his grip): Right?

Roy: I gotta cut him, Sal.

Sal: Right, kid?

Stevie: Yeah, right, right.

The tension eases a bit.

Sal: Sure, I thought so. You're Jewish, aren't you, kid?
Yes, no, maybe?
S (finally): Yes.
Sal: Then you're in luck, kid. My friend here's Jewish, too.
Roy's round face, an ambiguous smile.
Thunder and lightning, a fat raindrop. They let Stevie go.
Sal: See you around, asshole.
They go. Stevie takes a deep breath, shakes his head, smiles bitterly. Then he slaps his left-hand pocket.
A clank of coins.

"Awful the way the neighborhood's going to ruin, coloreds moving in."

I'm about to be invaded by Z and his *femme*. They think I've found an unspoiled spot, so they're flying down to spoil it. Besides, she's "just dying" to meet me. I'm supposed to be flattered and roll out the carpet when they come and, never mind the disruption, put on my best smiling face. Then we can all sit down, the three of us, cozy and snug, and talk about the project. Damn his impertinence!

What is the color of fear? A color code. Fear, safety, caution is yellow. Blue is the color of sorrow and loss, but also of sky, aspiration. The "blues." Red is somehow violent, the strong active emotions, love and hate, blood, exertion. Pink is feminine, a tincture of red. Black/brown is the earth, the depths, all that lies below. Gray reality, the artifice of pavement; burnish gray and it becomes silver. Black and white versus colors. Words, ideas: the rainbow confusion of dreams. Green is growth, the gray-green bushes behind the iron fence. In practice, of course, there must be no symbolism. It's all a matter of tone.

When it starts to rain, Stevie gives up waiting for Lester and decides to go home alone. That tropical storm. Plashing through the rain. Getting stuck on the subway. Crowds, everyone sweating, panic creeping in. A transformation. But how? This is all crap. Just one of those days, bleakness nagging me.

A mature, concurrent ploy, a counterpoint to Stevie. Leo Feuer simply won't do. He's too dim, too ignorant. Who then? Try to project yourself, grown, but somehow still living on Montgomery Street. What would you have to be? A failure. Youthful dreams and ambitions now thwarted. Has succumbed to the simplicity and security of the place. In-drawn, bitter. He lives in the past. He fixes things. "It's all I can do." Runs some sort of fix-it shop on Nostrand Avenue. A local character. The neighbors find him strange.

Grew up in the thirties. Politics. Was a Communist, then came the McCarthy era. His nonsensical idealism has done him in. He's literate, articulate. Married but childless. What would his wife be like? His impotent rage; has no outlets. The world has become too much for him. Too vivid, too cluttered—because he sees so well. Desire to retreat. The gun plot? A kind of Leo Feuer with brains and moxie.

Call him Max. Steen, Stein, Stone. M.S.

Why should I be interested in this guy, Z will want to know. Counterpoint.

Events which Stevie and Max each see just part of, almost subliminal actions, suggestions, of all the other stories that could be told about Montgomery Street. "There are eight million stories in the naked city." Willy is one. A girl being seduced by an older lesbian. Someone going crazy. Benny's alcoholism. Depression, anxiety, all sorts of symptoms. That new car. A marriage breaking up. Someone having a baby. Someone dying.

It's an election year. The lamp posts, the telephone poles,

billboards, trees, all littered with campaign posters. Not just Kennedy/Nixon but local stuff. Make it authentic. Find out who was running for what in Brooklyn that year.

Trees? What trees? That's the day they come to cut down the last tree on Montgomery Street, a diseased sycamore. Yellow truck, clamor of buzz saws, kids looking on. A tree dies in Brooklyn.

———

Playing versus working. The grownups of Montgomery Street have forgotten how to play. Thus the stupid earnestness of the place, the glum severity of earning a buck. Play versus games. To play is to imagine—let's pretend. You make up your own rules as you go along. While in games the rules are fixed. Life pushes us on from the freedom of playing to the arbitrary rules of gaming, and then on to working, where the arbitrary rules come to seem like absolutes. Childhood isn't innocent—it's burdened with nightmares—but it is, in a sense, our memory of the freedom we seek. Children can enter a make-believe world, know it's make-believe, and yet act as though it were reality. It's an act of imagination, and thus of empathy; to play together is to share fantasies and thus to join two lives. "Now you be the mommy and I'll be the daddy." Put young children together and you have instant community. Contrast this to the edginess of adolescents, who are preparing themselves to be grownups by giving up play for games.

Some grown-up character who is always playing, inventing realities around himself, breaking the rules, disrupting things. Everyone thinks he's mad. Somehow there has to come the recognition that life itself is a form of play, or at least ought to be—that we have invented the rules which make us ourselves and are only pretending that they're real. The recognition of how much of what we do is play is our sanity. The truly insane, the Willys, are always grim.

"Wanna play?"

"What's playing?"

In movies, in art of every kind, we get to watch someone else at play, inventing a world, a new set of rules. When it's good, we get to join in, we play along, become children again. The community of movie buffs.

So what else is new?

Z and J arrive in the morning and I'm just piddling away my time. I can't work for the waiting.

I should've known it. J turns out to have been the woman with pink hair. A wig is all it was, of course, part of the joke. "You looked like you wanted something romantic to happen to you." And the key? "I figured you'd send it back." Implying she wouldn't have minded if I hadn't. A liberated woman, no doubt about it, and thoroughly charming. The kind you can't take your eyes off. Which I suppose is why he brought her here. But he's a Philadelphia Zuckerman and doesn't know the difference between Brooklyn and Queens. She's Kew Gardens to the core, a product of professional parents and advantages and lawns. A cheerleader fallen among bohemians. I drove them around Sète and showed them the sights and she gushed, found it all so enchanting, so picturesque, so authentic. Z was more direct: "You mean to say you really like it here?"

Credit him, though. He has a sharp eye and sound instincts and possibly even the remnants of a soul within that gaudy leisure suit.

But did I manage to sell him?

We had dinner in "my" restaurant and talked about the project. God, how I talked! I did Montgomery Street for them, pushing around spoons and glasses and mussel shells, trying to bring it to life; I made it sound as epic and commercial as *Gone With the Wind*. And he sat there and listened and never said a word. "You know me, I have to see it on paper." So I promised him a treatment by the end of the month.

Anyway, they've been and gone, having stolen just one day. But I can't help suspecting that somehow they've destroyed this place for me, took the memories and life out of it, the way filming on location does. Orson Welles on Venice: "Now it's just a movie set." Maybe it's just that I've had to look at it for a moment through new eyes, their eyes. Damn them! They've made me feel far away from Brooklyn. It'll take a while to get back.

———

Bono's life, that self-contained solitude, is a result of his stasis. To be with others, to be in a community of any kind, implies accepting the possibility of change—that others can change you. Hence, Max.

———

Maxie Stein. He's forty-one years old. Stevie in a mirror.

———

I suspect she's a natural, that she can project herself without seeming to. She's strong, and she's managed to make herself interesting; she lives and breathes this self she has chosen to be, and she'll go on living and breathing it in front of a camera as easily as in a restaurant. A marvelous creation. Where has she been? How come I haven't heard of her before? She must be at least thirty; she's no starlet, no ingénue.

That she should insinuate herself into my thoughts, and so into the project, is just what Z planned. But putting her in means going off on some kind of tangent. I would have to expand my conception to contain her, or somehow shrink her down to M. St. size.

———

Stevie on that subway. Stuck in a tunnel. Floods up ahead. The way the train crawls, stops, lurches, crawls some more. Then the motor shuts off, the lights blink. The people around him, panic setting in. It seems to him that he's immune, superior. But how to show it? He sees the beast in them. Bah!

———

Max has some kind of artsy hobby. Carvings. He has whittled a set of figurines, replicas of his neighbors, has created a whole little world about him, a miniature Montgomery Street, a Van Eyck mirror. Little carving of Stevie. What's their relationship? Is he Maxie's kid? No. How then do I bring them together?

———

Use her? How? She's definitely not the rabbi's wife. That precise network of lines on her face is a map of sophistication. Could she do somehow for Max? His wife? His mistress? Does he have a mistress? Hard to imagine.

But there's the problem. Put her in and everything will tend to gravitate toward her until she's at the center. It would be a struggle—but would the struggle not be creative? Fascinating creature, she really is. That dancer's suppleness. I suppose in the background there's a childhood of ballet lessons, a pushy mother—and then she grew too tall. It's her size that does it, and the way her energy spills out in enthusiasms and superstitions. Her skin is either a masterwork of artifice or a stroke of genetic luck. The way she sings to herself when she's bored, singing inside her head, drumming her fingers. Her deadpan imitation of Lauren Bacall—some of that same quality, cool, husky-voiced—but then something else breaks through like a sun through cloud, and the iciness is gone. The way she sits with her legs pulled up under her, not quite the lotus position because the knees are too high, with her elbows thrust out sharply and her head in her hands. An inch more here or there and the effect would become grotesque, the freakish ugliness of a contortionist; but she never goes that far. It's all range and flexibility. And the next moment she can curl up and seem as soft and round and boneless as a kitten. Fascinating combination. Plenty of curve, lots of bone structure.

She burns herself into the mind like an afterimage. Star quality. But to imagine her on Montgomery Street is to imagine a leopard in a dog pound. Chance it?

Wonder what she has going with Z.

Stevie on the subway. Whether to make it the turning point or just another incident. How much plot do I need? How much can I rely on the texture of people, places? Still can't seem to picture it.

Forget her. Do Max. Then we'll see.

Max is in his store, working, when a girl passes by his window. He catches only a glimpse of her, and is nonetheless stricken by her loveliness, or what seems to be her loveliness: a peripheral impression of dark hair, tan skin, white dress, bare arms. It excites him, his impulse is to run after her, but he doesn't. He sits there wondering how much of that loveliness was real, how much has he only imagined. Better, he believes, to hang on to the image, unviolated by reality. For him the world is a series of hints upon which imaginings may feast and grow. Too much perception may destroy.

All day long people keep telling him he reminds them of someone they know. "Haven't we met before?" "Didn't you used to live on Fulton Street?" "You look exactly, but exactly, like an uncle of mine." There is, in fact, a brotherhood of short, swarthy, bald men of which Max is a member. But he rebels against being an example of a universal and familiar type. Ends up looking in a mirror, wondering whether he reminds himself of someone *he* knows. "Well, maybe I do look a little like X, but the differences are crucial!" Nonetheless, he begins to suspect that there exists beneath the apparent randomness of things a secret pattern he cannot ascertain.

The mystery of hidden order, Max on the verge of religion.

When you stare at yourself in a mirror for too long, your own face can startle you, rearrange itself, become strange and new.

49

Same with words repeated over and over again. Same with places—as when you come home after a vacation. Because we never really see the world; even our own face in a mirror is a mind-spun form of a face and not a nose, lips, eyes themselves. In other words, we look at the world through our memories, memories of the forms the world once took for us, and only with effort can we surrender to reality. Thus I now hold in my mind an image of J which will superimpose itself the next time we meet upon whatever she happens to look like, whatever she happens to be. And that's why perception can destroy. The world is strange; the mind tries to make it familiar. A constant struggle. All of which is related to Stevie's experience on the subway, the problem of Max, the premises of "Montgomery Street."

For Stevie the street is a familiar place; in the course of that day he changes enough so that it becomes strange for him. He sees it fresh and new. Maybe Max is the opposite. For him it's always been strange, he lives in nervous tension—"What in heaven's name am I doing here?" In the course of his day, it jells, becomes familiar. Somehow I've got to find a way of suggesting both processes at once. That way I can transcend my own limitations, film not just *my* Montgomery Street, but Montgomery Street itself, caught, fixed by a process of triangulation.

To know anything of substance about the world requires a multiplicity of points of view, which is to say a multiplicity of selves. What, in fact, does the candy store look like through Bertie Grossman's eyes?

Transcending the morass of self. We are creatures who not only hope to find form in the mess of reality; what we constantly seek to do is hammer the mess into a shape that suits us, work at it until it comes to resemble those preconceived notions of form we bring to it. The forms we impose upon the world give us our sense of self. When we can't impose the forms, when the world remains intractably strange, we enter a stage of crisis. Because the world won't yield, we must; we are forced to change.

Stevie on the subway. Transformation, an altering of his sense of self, notions of who he is, notions derived from Montgomery Street. He is shoved willy-nilly through the doorway of adolescence into a new maturity (and consequently loses some of his power to play). The world around him remains what it was, but his mind now looks through new lenses, so to speak, so nothing he sees will ever seem quite the same again. Not even his own face in the mirror. He has left his childhood forever, quite flown away from it, and Montgomery Street. Though, of course, he will always have memories of what he's been, and these keep him from solipsism.

Because there is a world out there, and even though we impose upon it, it may have patterns of its own.

That's why Max comes eventually to flirt with religion.

All of which is rather abstract, no?

Don't sell your story for a mess of philosophy.

Dramatize!

The point is it must be made fearsome and exhilarating. Stevie learns that we are all many selves from day to day, and yet we are also the same—the way a movie star, a Bogart, a Redford, is both himself and also the roles he plays from film to film. Which jars him, wrenches him into a new connection to everything around him, friends, neighbors, parents, the street itself, like that moment in *Ivan the Terrible* when the film bursts into color. Eisenstein, having imposed a stark and shadowy vision upon us, reminds us how arbitrary and artificial any vision is. A formalist to the end. Snubbing his nose at Stalin, I suppose. Revolutionary grandeur? Realism for the proletariat? Don't forget, folks, it's just a bit of film.

Find some equivalent for Stevie on the subway. Change tone, shape, textures. Do it with sound track? A distorting lens? Is there such a thing as a nondistorting lens?

Play, then, with the conventions of film, that Hollywood desire to soothe by making everything familiar.

Too ambitious? Why not dream?

———

Max is tactile, Stevie visual. He—

———

Max: "Just turn the screws a bit, put pressure on a man, and the next thing you know he'll be spouting abstractions, pomposities, just like a politician."

———

Max runs an antique store, but he can't quite make a living at it, so he subsidizes the business by fixing things: toasters, electric mixers, broken clocks. He loves to work with his hands; he loves having the pieces of a thing spread out on a table in front of him, the joy of putting together disassembled parts. Plug it in: will it work? Gears, wheels, rheostats, transformers. You don't have to think about it, you just do it. His store is a clutter of antiques, relics, objects seen through a haze of nostalgia, mostly junk. Bedraggled furniture, china dolls, stereopticons. They become a clue to his thoughts, the merely mental laid out in front of us in a series of objects. What objects? War posters. Old coins, too valuable to spend. Gone-with-the-wind lamps. Carnival glass. A toy savings bank: hunter shoots dime into bear. An artificial nigger. Piles of old magazines. *National Geographics.* Poor Max always wanted to travel, see the world, but he has a young and lively and expensive wife. How would they have gotten together? If he's man enough for her, what would he be doing on Montgomery Street?

———

Their apartment is a battleground upon which her spontaneity struggles with his need for order. Those carvings of his are all over the place. Some are arranged on the shelves of a bookcase, others on a glass tabletop. Tiny creatures with big eyes, gaping mouths, jutting chins. They're grouped into scenes: a wedding, a drunken brawl, kids at play. A bearded old specimen lies sleeping in a doll's bed, beneath a doll's quilt, atop the television. Another dangles like a fallen mountain climber from a cord looped over the radiator knob.

This has to be done right. Budget line for it. Tell Mort.

They're all carved out of soap!

Different brands, colors. Max can tell someone about the texture of Ivory, the feel of Camay. Yellow, green, pink. The figure of a bride carved from a bar of pale amber transparent beauty soap, a labor of love, the image his wife has separated herself from.

He has used the most homey and accessible materials to decorate the things, give them a semblance of life. Rags made into clothes; hair from a hunk of stuffing pulled from a hole in the sofa.

We watch Max at work. Chips of plaster from a peeling wall he uses to carve teeth. His workroom—the kitchen? (His wife hates to cook?) He has dozens of X-Acto knives, a secondhand dentist's drill with lots of attachments—bits, grinders, polishers.

He lectures someone on the virtues of competing brands. "Best is Lux!"

They're grotesque little things with huge heads and shrunken bodies: in the dim evening light they seem nastily animated, watching Max with accusing eyes.

There's a leak in the ceiling. "One good rainstorm and I'll end up with nothing but suds and bubbles."

They're satiric renderings of his neighbors, portraits of ugliness, meanness, smallness. They haunt him. His mind has rebelled against the plain malicious truths his hands have created.

He's ashamed of them. He keeps them in boxes, out of sight, in case a neighbor drops in.

He has tried to carve images of beauty and pleasure, but he has no talent for it.

He's an insomniac. He works instead of sleeps. He loves the carving itself, the absorption of it, the privacy, the intimacy, the dry softness of the soap on his hands, the way the stuff yields to the keen blade. But in his hands it all turns to pain, beauty becomes grotesque. Tries to explain this to someone. A mistress? His discontent.

Thoughts of suicide. His fear of these thoughts.

Max in love?

———

Stevie builds model airplanes. Big red Fokker triplane hanging in his room. But he's not very good at it. He always seems to botch the job; can't make materials yield up the image he sees. His worktable spread with newspaper. Balsa wood, glue. The mess of it spreading from his room to the rest of the apartment. His mother complains. "Just look at the mess you're dragging in!" Razor blades, dope, silkscreen. Marvelous stuff.

———

Maybe the point is they never do come together, never intersect. Two ways of looking at Montgomery Street, mutually exclusive. Matter and antimatter. Some intermediary then?

———

Stevie must come to terms with his fear of life, passion, sex, freedom: we see him becoming the man he will be. Max's is a middle-age crisis; he must come to terms with death. He was there when the old woman jumped off the roof. He was the one who finally hosed down the sidewalk. Remember that, despite his struggles, in a crisis he's strong, and the neighbors instinctively turn to him.

Do that scene, that death plunge I'll never forget? Let it be part of that Friday?

No, it's happened earlier and he's been brooding about it. We get flickers of it, a couple of frames at a time. He remembers it, how he caught a glimpse of her hobbled climb up onto the retaining wall, her moment of hesitation that must have been all doubt and wonder, her desperate conviction, and then the fall itself, tumbling down silently, like a bundle of rags. Why didn't she scream? Then the thump of sparse flesh and bone on the sidewalk in front of Korski's, and having to hose down the mess, and a municipal ambulance, in no hurry at all, pulling away. A crowd gathering, kids talking about it, a short chubby kid showing his lanky pal where a piece of skull has landed: it takes Montgomery Street no more than a few minutes to transform what Max believes to be an act of courage into an Abbott and Costello routine.

Max on the roof, taunting himself, tantalizing his fears. "Go on, fly!"

Why did she do it? One of those mysteries I never solved. Must have been suffering from some excruciating and terminal disease.

"Life's a terminal disease," Max tells someone.

So he's haunted. He knows that we are all capable of suicide under certain conditions of stress, and he has come to believe that, seen baldly, life is hardly worth the struggle. At first these thoughts just buzz on the surface of his mind; but then they stick and feed and fatten into a kind of panic. The crisis comes that Friday. He finds the gun? "I'm going to do it," he keeps telling himself, "I'm going to do it." He believes it won't be a rational decision but just an impulse. Real suicide isn't something you have to plan. You don't have to be pushed to it; you merely leap. Into a momentary void between two disconnected thoughts death comes.

"Which is why you hear later that they didn't bother to cancel their appointments, or that they left their breakfasts half-eaten when they turned on the gas."

Scary, isn't it?

For Max the question becomes bleak and terrifying: It has happened to others, why not me? Finding the gun pushes him from speculation to the need for decision.

A day filled with death. He goes off to Brownsville to buy up the furniture of some old couple that died. The suburban son. "Just make me a reasonable offer." Max reading the obituaries:

he's reached that age. Headlines filled with murder, war, accidents. A funeral procession goes by. He smashes a silverfish with a rolled-up newspaper. He's squeamish about it. Memories of his dead parents. Korski, the concentration camps. In the evening a neighbor has a heart attack. Max goes with him to the hospital. In the waiting room of the emergency ward, the bustle that surrounds death, the strange complacencies of torn flesh, a crisis coming on.

Dom is dying.

"He saw the skull beneath the skin."

Dying generations.

On television someone is talking about the Dead Sea Scrolls.

Kids fighting: "Give it back or I'll kill you."

He harbors within himself, he believes, a maniacal murderer whose intended victim is himself.

What's making me so morbid?

———

His energetic wife is too much for him. An affair. He's been cuckolded. The shame of it. But that makes him too pathetic. I want a strong bold Max. Can't seem to get him in focus. Too close to him. Stevie's okay because I'm no longer him, no longer only him, anyway; but I seem to be concocting Max out of the worst parts of me. Last year's crisis. Thought I was through it. Bad time last night, my heart pounding. Why? Maybe I've had enough of this place, enough of being alone. Home to New York? Z said I should come meet them in London. Can't quite figure his game. What does he expect of me? In any case, I want to have this thing more clearly in mind before I go. A week more. Maybe two.

———

Max's carving. Intercut pan of them with pan of street at some busy moment. Chinese boxes.

———

I have focused too much on Stevie and Max and have lost sight of the street itself. Remember: that's at the center of it. I've been

56

doing too much imagining, not enough remembering; gotten too tight with it, letting it jell too soon. The way those memories came a couple of weeks ago now seems like a visitation. There's more there, has to be, and I have to relax enough to reach it, unearth it.

On the other hand, I may already have more material than I know what to do with.

Toward evening, a menacing car, two burly black men. Are they going to rob the candy store?

Shlemmer, the butcher, the third store on the block. His pinkie missing. How we said he lost it in the grinder, sold it as chopped meat. His son, the allergy doctor—meeting Michelle in the waiting room, our mutual shame. BB guns, giving someone a pink belly. The way my father always wore a white shirt and tie to go off to the factory, no working-class hero he. Irwin's cousin who joined the army to get his flat feet fixed. The scroll of war dead near Nostrand Avenue. The time we sat in the schoolyard watching Ruthie undress. Knew we were there, the bitch. Those people in 500, two brothers and a sister, the Uglies we called them, a strange triangle. The garage on New York Avenue with the nude calendars and how the men came with a wrench to chase us away. High Holidays when we made blackjacks out of rolled-up hankies and ran around like maniacs ruining our best clothes. A sign in Max's store: "Today's Junk is Tomorrow's Treasure!"

Max the old radical: "Working class? There is no working class any more. Nowadays everyone dresses like a boss, thinks like a boss. Which leaves only the coloreds. What kind of revolution is that for me?"

Max waking up. His wife sleeping next to him. Skip her for now.

57

The bathroom: Max enters and turns on the light. He's in his underwear, blinking, squinting. Have to hold him at a comic distance. He pees. A waist shot: but on the sound track the unmistakable hiss of his urine down into the toilet bowl, rainbow's end. He's a bald, dark-cheeked man with a red boil ablaze on his forehead. Hairy. A jungle of hair overflows the sagging neckline of his dingy undershirt. One of those bald men who seem to have an excess of hormones, the myth of their virility. Long arms, slumped shoulders, a slightly gibbonish look. We see him first, then, barefoot and scratching: image of a large gentle beast of a man with brooding intelligent eyes.

Shakes himself off. Tone is everything. He glances at his rumpled angry face in the medicine chest mirror, rinses his hands, raises a wet forefinger to his reflection and shoots himself, pow, pow, pow, just like that. Then he brushes his teeth with the same finger. He smokes cigars: awful the morning taste of a cigar smoker's mouth. But he can't stomach the thought of toothpaste. A kind of hangover, but not from booze. He's had a bad night.

He coughs, a small convulsion of coughing, snuffles, spits a brownish mess into the sink. Close-up: we see it whirl in the water and vanish. The point is to find just the right proportion of disgust, the mess of life. Make their bellies churn a bit, force a nervous laugh, but don't sicken them. Realism so real, etc.

In the bedroom. His wife sleeping sprawled diagonally across the bed, blanket bundled around her. We suspect she's taken his space, squeezed him out. Something sensuous about her sleeping there.

Bed scenes are always hard to do. In movies no one ever wakes up with pillow creases pressed onto their faces, that morning map of night's excursion; they never have gook in their mouths, sand in their eyes; they don't smell of their sleep and dreams. This is the kind of detail you must pay attention to. It's what the world is made of.

The living room. Those figurines. Some antiques. Magazines. Emblems of his wife's tastes.

Goes to the window, looks down through the curtains at Montgomery Street. Seven o'clock. Korski, Jeremy, Stevie running in the schoolyard. Those church bells.

How to handle time? Make the actions synchronous? Easier to make them sequential. Avoid the complications of going back and forth in time. Don't want to confuse them. Or do I?

He's restless. Doesn't know what to do with himself. Why did he get up so early? His wife in her stirring nudged him out of sleep. Examines the pattern of cracks in the ceiling. Settles on the sofa, resting his head against a cushion. Up again to turn on the television. *Sunrise Semester*. Someone lecturing on the Dead Sea Scrolls.

He has stooped to turn on the TV. When he stands up again, the blood rushes out of his head. For a moment he is dizzy, sweating, afraid he's dying.

No good.

I seem to see him all right but I can't feel him acting. I don't have the pulse of his life. Because I can't do him without doing her. They define each other.

———

There are people who tend to believe what they see and people who don't. People for whom the objects of sight are real and solid, and people for whom these same objects, a chair, a gun, a mirror, are transitory and slippery, mere shadows of something else. The former tend to act upon experience, the latter upon abstractions. The former live in the world, the latter in their minds. Bono lives too much in the world, Stevie too much in imagination. How does Max fit in?

———

Don't forget the importance of music, how I used to solace myself. Sound track made up of bits and pieces of the songs of the day. Integrate it. Max, of course, likes classical music, Bach and Mozart, hates Chopin. He keeps a radio going in the shop, loses himself in the music, starts to conduct.

Stevie's just old enough to remember the origins of rock 'n' roll, and smart enough to understand how they killed it, the big money men. Connects to the civil rights movement, the fear of blacks moving in. He has a collection of 45s, golden oldies, Chuck Berry, Little Richard. In 1960 it's all gone. Elvis is in the army with his hair cut off.

The importance of hair. In Stevie's society of boys, the style of your hair is a vital assertion.

Why is he so much more fun to do than Max?

His room. A bed, a desk, lots of books. The Hardy Boys. Tarzan. Clair Bee novels. Some science fiction from the library. (Yellow stripes for sf, red for mysteries.) *The Conquest of Mexico.* Picture book about World War II. Clues to his mind. Comic books: *Captain Marvel, Tales from the Crypt.* Classic comics: *Black Beauty, The Odyssey, The Three Musketeers.* That big red Fokker triplane. All troubles come in threes. A bridge table on which is spread the bits and pieces of his latest project, a ribbed wing, squeezed tubes of glue, old paintbrushes, a soft dusting of balsa wood. What else? Bats, balls. Still a Dodger fan? Picture of Sandy Koufax, Jewish athlete, practically an oxymoron. The wallpaper is old and stained, a remnant of his childhood. Cowboys and Indians in the pattern, or maybe little pale-blue teddy bears on toy merry-go-rounds. Games: Monopoly, Ghost, Clue. His parents watching TV in the living room.

Separate them from mine.

They're old, very old. He's a menopausal child.

Remember the Blooms?

His father's a big tall man, sixtyish, a housepainter. Over the years the chalky whiteness of plaster has settled into his skin, his hands, his horny fingernails. Against this whiteness—he's a kind of plaster saint—his eyes seem extraordinarily wet, red-rimmed.

His talk is accented by his native Russia, which he fled as a boy. To avoid the Czar's army. He came to America with nothing but a single gold coin which he carried hidden in his shoe. Likes to reminisce about it. (Scene with Max?) How he managed never to spend it. Still carries it with him, an amulet, a charm. Fishes it out of his pocket. Eroded by time, it gleams in his dry hand like a small sun. A bright memory gleaming in a laborious life.

The mother—is Feuer still the name? She's a short, round, bustling sort of woman with henna-dyed hair. Salt of the earth, the people God made the world for. Old-fashioned, heartsick knowing that their traditions will die with them. They have childhood memories of the old world, have never quite adjusted to the new.

Stevie's problem then is, in part, that he was raised by people who are most like other kids' grandparents. Thus his shyness, his bookishness, his awkwardness, his sexual naïveté, his air of having been pampered, his unworldliness, his dreams, his fiery ambitions.

He is, in his own mind, a kind of orphan.

He is also, deep down, aware of ancient sanctities, of connection to a past that his third-generation friends can never know. Custom, form, ceremony. He struggles, he kicks, but he simply cannot be as cynical as Lester is.

Fantasy that he's a foundling, a secret prince. The shame of it. He belongs, spiritually, to another world. His impossible yearning. The way I used to cringe when I came to the place-of-birth line on some application, some form to fill out.

Are you Jewish, kid?

Yes!

We see the Feuers walking together on Montgomery Street, a heart-gladdening sight. The tall strong slab of him, so erect and solid; the soft round bobbing ball of her, chattering at his side. An image of all we've lost.

But they can't help Stevie through his current crisis.

Has breakfast with his mother. She dotes on him, but just can't understand.

"You have to get up so early? You have to knock yourself out? Tell me, where does it get you? What do you hope to achieve?"

Stevie's sullen silence.

———

Stevie on the subway. It doesn't have to be a big deal, an epiphany. It's just another phase of the crisis coming on. Images of all his parents have tried to protect him from. A blind man playing an accordion, his blank blue bulging eyes rolling in his head. A couple of young Wall Street types talking lewdly about some "piece of ass." Discarded newspapers. Half-scrubbed remains of a wino's piss and vomit on the floor. A sluttish teen-age girl pressing up against him, her breast on his arm. His first impulse is to move away, but she maneuvers to keep it there, exciting him, mesmerizing him—all the while she's chewing gum and staring at the advertisements overhead. At the next stop, she's gone. There are floods up ahead. The train stops, starts, stops, jerking everyone back and forth. People drenched by rain and sweat. Alternate voices and silence. The pulse of an idling engine. The way people suddenly become aware of themselves talking, breathing. An old woman, vaguely reminiscent of his mother, slowly becomes hysterical. Everyone becoming aware of their crucial isolation. The way you look around for someone to smile at. The ads. Double your pleasure, double your fun. If u cn rd ths u r rdy 4 a btr jb. The old woman faints. He can't do a thing about it. Faces under pressure. The way a veil seems to slip away, all the inner turmoil coming out. The shared relief when, finally, the train begins to move.

Keep it as simple as you can. It won't be an easy sequence to do.

———

Cut from Max to Stevie arriving home in the rain, running, no, not running, just walking along Montgomery Street, soaking wet.

Keep these scenes short, terse; find the right rhythm, the proper balance between Stevie and Max.

Scolded by Mama. She makes him undress, sets his clothes on a radiator, rubs him down with a towel, her baby, her *schatzeleh*.

"So where you been, mister?"

"Went to the movies."

"And what did you see?"

"Some dumb cowboy picture."

"This picture had a name?"

"Sure."

"So what was the name."

"I don't remember."

"You don't remember?"

"Will you stop babying me!"

"Why should I stop babying you? To me you're still a baby. Come in the kitchen, I make you some tea."

Don't make her a villain. She has a sense of humor; somehow she understands. Which for Stevie, of course, just makes it all seem worse.

———

Stevie, Max. Moving back and forth between the two of them will be easy enough. But add J and the structure may fall apart. The problem of keeping three separate lines moving simultaneously without being too mechanical. Unless she can be kept subordinate to one or the other, or both. Maybe find a way to create the illusion of an important role without giving her too much time on the screen. She hovers constantly in the background. She'll love that.

Will Z insist on her? He's made it clear he will. Why? I bet there's less there than meets the eye.

I can always write her into the script, close the deal, then go film it my way.

If I can finagle the final cut.

The schoolyard, evening. Establishing shot: we are looking down on it from a roof. The ambience is Breughelesque. Children's games. A cherry bomb booms in a garbage can. Kids playing stickball in the fading light. The rain has stopped, a September coolness has settled in. Strings of ladyfingers sputtering. Some girls clustered near a fence, watching what is essentially a boys' world. A father having a catch with his little boy, something Stevie never had. The kid's maybe five, six, but Dad is out to make him an athlete. Pressure. He's disappointed by the kid's lack of coordination. Ends up angry. We are zooming in slowly. Firecrackers explode. A kid throws a firecracker into another kid's pocket and a fight breaks out. Teen-agers with a transistor radio, some good old rock beat, Chuck Berry—

Hail! hail! rock 'n' roll!
Deliver me from the days of old!

Handicapped kids. A kid with crutches, a kid with a brace on his leg, Jeremy.

We pick Lester out of the crowd. He is selling firecrackers out of the saddlebag of his bike, a Schwinn Phantom with gleaming chrome fenders. Can you get a mirror shot from them? It should be a superb bike: crash bars, streamers, multiple reflectors. Lester the entrepreneur is attracting a crowd.

Jeremy is hanging around trying to get Lester to give him a firecracker.

"Please, Lester, just give me one, Lester, I'll pay you back, Lester, just one." In that whiny mongoloid singsong.

"Get the hell away from me, you crazy freak."

Establish Spider, hovering in the background. He's a hulking kid with a lantern jaw which he already shaves. Baggy gabardine pants, a white shirt, clothes obviously chosen by an overweening mom. Quirkish, shy, with a stupid amiable smile, he's there on the periphery. A misaimed ball rolls to his feet, he bends over, picks it up, throws it girlishly. A firecracker explodes near him; he hides his face in his arms, then smiles even more, trying to turn his fear into a joke. But for the moment no one is watching him. His hair is cut short and ragged, perhaps a home haircut. (Hair as definition: what happens when, like Max, you're bald?) One of the toughest-looking kids, passing by Spider, maliciously throws him a kiss, grabs at his crotch, laughs. Spider cringes.

Across the street one of the *yentehs* has been hanging out the window, watching. She shakes her head, disappears. Perhaps we can glimpse her in her apartment phoning the cops.

Pan: smoke in the air from the firecrackers, teen-agers' cigarettes, punks. Kids rolling hoops, playing tag, potsy, Johnny-on-the-pony. That tough-looking kid pulls a pack of obscene-backed playing cards from his pocket and gathers his own little crowd. An eight-year-old in a cowboy suit shoots everyone around him. Other kids are throwing rocks, trying to break the few remaining school windows.

Stevie arrives. We see him first in the background, wearing long pants and a zippered windbreaker, looking quite a bit older than he had in the morning. The girls near the fence say hello to him; he gets a smile from Anita, who's wearing a yellow sweater. Without even thinking about it, she takes a deep breath, swelling the sweater, but Stevie is preoccupied.

He goes to Lester, determined to be forceful, but Lester give him a bland smile, and pre-empts him.

L: Hey, partner, I looked all over for you.

S: Where the hell did you disappear to?

L (all innocence): Me? I came back and you were gone.

S (deflated): A couple of guys took money off me. Did you expect me to stand there forever?

They are interrupted by a small boy who offers Lester coins: Gimme two packs.

Then Bono comes through the schoolyard. For a moment the scene seems to swirl around him. He regards everything with humor and indulgence. He's in his element. A few kids come running up to him.

"Hi, Bono!" "How ya doing, Bono?" "Hey, Bono, watch me!"

Bono rumples the hair of the kid in the cowboy suit. Another boy grabs Bono's hand with both of his and Bono swings him around. Stevie watches it all a bit enviously. Bono never rumpled *his* hair, swung *him* around.

L: How much did they take off of you?

S: Maybe half a buck.

L: Forget it. You're going to be a rich man tonight.

Lester's hands, passing out packets of firecrackers, receiving coins. Bright paper packets, dragons on the labels.

Stevie eyes the take.

Then a siren in the distance.

Stevie. Lester, Back to Stevie, panic on his face.

The siren comes closer. Lester shoves firecrackers and money back into the saddlebag just as a cop car pulls into the schoolyard from the Crown Street side, red lights spinning, siren dying away.

Lester remains cool, an almost supercilious look on his face. Stevie looks around as though he wants to huddle against someone else; he feels alone, exposed.

Cop leaning out of the window, to Lester: Come over here.

L: Me?

Cop: I said get over here.

In the background: "What's a penny made out of? What's a dirty penny made out of?"

Meanwhile the second cop has gotten out of the car and comes around toward Stevie. He had stupid eyes, red ears. He looks from face to face.

First cop to L: You been selling firecrackers?

L: No.

Cop: You sure about that?

The second cop has read Stevie's face. He looks at the bike, back to Stevie, staring at him. For a long tense moment Stevie stands there struggling with himself—and then, after a day of guilt and shame, he breaks. Panicked, fleeing his private ghosts, he turns and runs.

Second cop: You little sonuvabitch!

Stevie running, the cop going after him.

The first cop getting out of the car, also going after him.

Lester on his bike goes off in the other direction.

Stevie flees down the schoolyard steps, across Montgomery Street (reverse of the morning shot).

The cop gets delayed when he stumbles over some little kid. This makes him so mad he pulls his gun.

Cop: Stop, you mother—

Stevie glancing back sees the cop has his gun out. His panic now becomes ferocious. He runs into one of the apartment buildings, not his own. Through the lobby, side-stepping a tricycle, toward the back.

The cop in the lobby trips over the tricycle, almost goes sprawling. By the time he's up again, his partner has arrived.

Second cop: That little—

First cop grabs him: You planning to shoot the kid for selling firecrackers?

Second cop, tight on his face as he realizes he's been a fool. He puts the gun away and gives up the chase.

But Stevie doesn't know this. He plunges through that maze of cellars and alleys and courtyards which make a kind of second, hidden Montgomery Street, interconnected, as labyrinthine as a good tale. He runs in and out of doors, up and down stairways, and there's no one chasing him, he's fleeing his own shadow, there's nothing behind him at all.

Finally he can run no more. Breathless, red in the face, he hides in a cellar. Cats, filth. At any moment the drunken janitor might catch him, fearsome James who was said to catch squirrels and cook them. "Little boys, too." Establish earlier that the cellar

67

is James's realm, a kingdom of bogeys, part of Stevie's nightmare now.

You can do more with the cellars and alleyways. It's where Stevie spent his boyhood, a private world. He knows all the ins and outs. Because it's familiar to him, strange to others, he feels protected there, in control, invulnerable. Perhaps have him and Lester talking about it, how, say, if a war broke out, they could hide there, harass the enemy, never be found.

Puddles, clogged sewers after that storm. Max throws a couple of pebbles into the dirty water, watches the oily rainbowed surface come alive with intersecting ripples.

Stevie climbs a back fence, goes through the lane where Dom lives, past the synagogue, shies away from the police station, walks through the darkening neighborhood, ends up on Crown Street, peeping in a window, seeing the *Hasidim* dance.

Theirs is a warm, closed, and rounded world, the antithesis of the cold, open-ended and ragged universe that Stevie is beginning to perceive. But how do you show a kid picking up impressions which will only much later in his life harden into the artifices of thought? Stevie is bright, but I don't want to make him precociously articulate, the way Hollywood versions of children usually are. The pathos of Montgomery Street is inarticulation. It senses but never really knows its hidden despairs, its hungers, its secret joys. In the course of that day Stevie will see everything but learn nothing. It registers, it's food for thought, but he won't be able to digest it until much later on.

Problem: how to imply the kind of man he will become? Through Max? But except in the vaguest way he won't end up like Max because in his future there'll be no Montgomery Street to flee to, no Montgomery Street to define him. How will he turn out then? What will he be? The maker of the film—that simple device? No, because I've pushed him off so far, distorted so much, that he's no longer me. I was fourteen three years earlier, and those three years were crucial. So he's not me, he's only an alternative imagined me. Imagination may be nothing more than the rearranging of remembered experience into new forms, but the newness of the form is everything.

A paradox. I've made Stevie up out of bits of my life, but Stevie's not me. How can I use it?

Where is Stevie going? Where am I taking him? And why?

The running, the rabbi's wife, being cheated, being robbed, the subway, the chase scene—one by one the confines of community are slipping away from him, he's being thrust toward the possibility of freedom.

What will he do with it? What happens to him at that moment of solitude when he realized he needn't be what the circle of friends, family, neighbors want him to be?

There are too many alternatives.

What if I had never married, lived those other kinds of life I chose to spurn? How would I have turned out? Would I still be making movies? Maybe, but they'd be artsy things, shot in 16mm and edited with a razor blade; or avant-gardish essays in pure form and movement, patterns scratched on blank stock with colored pens. I came close to going that way, after all—and if I had, everything around me, all that I see, would be totally different.

Regrets?

The point is that to choose is to bifurcate the world. The road not taken. The life we haven't chosen coexists with the life we have, at least in imagination. Of course one has regrets: one is always confronted with the maze of possible worlds, the might-have-beens.

We are always freer than we want to believe.

Suggest the plurality of worlds Stevie might someday inhabit. I don't have to know how he'll end up because I can think of dozens of possibilities. He may die in Vietnam or live to happy old age in Saskatchewan, become a fat accountant in Great Neck or a hairy poet on Avenue D. The point is the freedom he achieves. Open the closed form of conventional narrative; suggest the essential fluidity of experience, the freedom that's ours for the taking. We make up our lives as we go along; from moment to moment we can be whatever we want to be. So long as you keep struggling against circumstance and upbringing; so long as you don't get trapped by Montgomery Street.

Tense this morning. Trying to keep hold of the thread of the thing is making me tense. Why? Because it all seems too simple, too glib. Freedom is ours for the taking? We can be whatever we want to be? How easy it is to slip into sentimentality, banal optimism. And all because I want praise, a pat on the head, a big success. Message as merchandise, the illusion they crave. The smell of money is in it. Stevie in that cellar isn't free; he's panicked, terrified, and will grab hold of the first solid thing that comes along. The way I grabbed Ellie, the way we always slink off to the nearest cage.

No, that's not right either. That's just morning gloom.

Stevie in the cellar: how much freedom does he have?

We are nothing more than our memories of what we've been and our visions of what we're becoming—a remembered past, an imagined future, and the interplay of the two, the present moment, a struggle in the web of time. We go around like Alice with a chunk of mushroom in either hand, past and future, memory and imagination, a nibble here, a nibble there. . . .

Look at how passive I've made him. The point now is to propel him toward some action, a choice, a change.

Blank.

In movies, characters are always endlessly and tediously themselves. Which is nothing more than a convention borrowed from Victorian novels and melodramas, and reinforced by the necessities of the star system. But it's such a pervasive convention that we have mistaken it for life itself—we hang on to the familiar, what we've always been. The possibility of change is experienced as crisis.

Remember the panic I felt when I left E? That first night in the hotel, thirty floors up, and all I could think of was I should find myself a whore. Those awful weeks of transition, the feeling that some part of me was empty and I could choose to fill it with anything at all. Freedom—and I hated every minute of it. The nightsweats, the headaches, the way my heart would start pounding, the ringing in my ears, that sense of strangeness. Primordial, I suppose, the alarm system of a Neanderthal who has blundered into an alien neighborhood, far from his home cave. My edginess this morning, the way I woke up thinking I didn't have to go on being what I was, that I was nothing more than a series of quirks and habits, that I could give up being the old familiar Stephen Mandreg as easily as I gave up smoking.

But then what?

Imagination fails, the habit of self remains unbreakable. But the fact is that imagination is too vivid. Our quirks and jobs and hair styles are there to keep anxiety at bay, nerve endings sheathed. We stay ourselves, we choose to stay ourselves, because the alternatives frighten us. We are afraid that should we try to live our dreams, we may tumble into our nightmares.

Max with a gun: a murderer?

To relinquish the past is to flirt with madness.

Amnesia.

How as you're falling asleep the dream images sometimes start to come before the waking mind has relinquished its hold, how you come awake, startled, afraid for a moment that you don't know where you are, you've forgotten your name, you've lost yourself.

Amnesiacs, true amnesiacs, are rare, but all those old movies about amnesiacs are fascinating, sure-fire stuff, because we flirt with the possibility of it every night. We suspect that memory can vanish, and with it the tedious responsibility of going on with our lives. But the amnesiac always turns out to have forgotten nothing more than events and facts; he remains what he was—at least that's true of the Hollywood version of the amnesiac, and since that's the one we pay to see, that's the one that counts. Real psychotics in real asylums seldom interest us. The myth: he struggles to remember and eventually does; there comes that second knock on the head; he regains his identity—and we consider that a happy ending! Because behind it is the notion that we have an existence independent of our experience, a core, a soul. You can change the circumstances of your life, but you have to go on being yourself. How neat, how reassuring. We meet ourselves coming or going. Character is fate. Montgomery Street made me, thus I *am* Montgomery Street. Filming the neighbors to mirror me. If this is true, we really are stuck. But what if it's just an illusion, a way of calming our fears?

Reject it then. The alternative is freedom. You can be whatever you want to be. And the price of freedom is fear.

I was attracted to Stevie, age fourteen, because for an adolescent change comes willy-nilly. He can't go on being the child he was; he has to come to terms with his freedom. Which is why teen-agers tend to be such irritable lunatics. The crisis of being forced to change. Will Stevie merely ride it out or take it in hand, make himself new? Panic or possibility? Most people merely ride it out. Then they have to go off to confessors of one kind or another to find out what they were, discover what they are now supposed to be. The so-called identity crisis. The sense of drift and disconnection.

They go to movies to learn not just how to feel, but what to be. They want flashes of recognition. "Ah, so that's what I am!"

Someday Stevie will turn around and see that he has run and run right out of himself, out of childhood and the circle of his friends, out of Montgomery Street, the way a cartoon character runs off a cliff into midair. Then he can either scramble back or plummet.

At the critical moment, suspended there by nothing more than wishful thinking, he becomes an image of Max!

Max with the gun: will he let himself fall?

Stevie in the cellar. The mood is trepidation, but also exhilaration. He has entered the spookhouse of becoming. The point is the transition itself, like jumping off a roof or plunging through a mirror; for a crucial moment we step outside of memory and imagination, live totally in the present, and thus see the world as it is and not merely as a reflection of ourselves. The clarity and starkness of a camera lens. Those are the moments film is meant to show.

So then, you can change, the freedom is there.

Stevie is plunged into the anxiety of freedom. How much courage does he have; how much courage can I give him?

———

Can't seem to shake the mood. I seem to be sitting here watching my life unreel, biting my nails, afraid of what I might see next. All week I've had London on my mind. Go to London, let Z shove you back in line, keep you from being too artsy. After all, he's the mirror in which I can see the familiar Stephen Mandreg I've become. The comforting armor of routine, repetition, imitative style. The bland reassurances of technical skill. But technical skill is not enough. Which is why, deep down, the success of *Centerpeice* keeps nagging at me. It's not a movie I would have admired when I was nineteen. It's too slick, glib, cynical. I don't want to have to go on being forever the Stephen Mandreg I was

73

when I made it. On the other hand, coming to Sète was more of an escape than I planned.

My choice now.

I don't want to deny what I've been. I don't hate my past that much. And I don't want to waste what I know. The fact that those plain hard-earned technical skills are not enough doesn't make them worthless.

There, that's the Max in me.

You may fall asleep believing you have no name; in your dreams you may be anything at all, moving through worlds that are limitless and bizarre; but then morning comes round at last and you find you are still sane and whole after all. Don't glorify that surrender of self, which is more breakdown than freedom.

Max won't commit suicide; he won't even come close.

———

Stevie, then, is a story of change, Max a story of stasis. No, that's still not right. Max rather is a story of resistance to change. Somehow he's gotten stuck in the past, lives too much in memory. His imagination has been thwarted. He has to get dragged kicking and screaming into a new sense of self. How? What events? A woman? Do Stevie and Max meet? Where? When? In what way can they possibly connect?

———

With Stevie the visual style must change as he goes along. Possibly even use different stocks, get grainier toward the end. The final freeze shot in *400 Blows*, when we see the man the kid has become. The last image of Stevie should somehow echo initial image of Max. He pees before he goes to bed. But beware the mere prettiness of symmetry. Change color values. Maybe start with muted gray tones; make them brighter, more saturated and vivid as we go along. Or the opposite. We go from day to night, spring to autumn, youth to age.

———

The desire to be Bono is the desire for stability, permanent youth.

It's a trap that leads to the rot of Dom. Stevie breaks the circle, accepts change, allows himself to go off, so to speak, on a tangent. In the end he envies Bono not at all.

Nostalgia is a symptom of dread. Don't cater to it.

Stevie returns to Montgomery Street. What now? How will he be received after what has happened with the cop? He's afraid to go home: do his parents know?

Maybe the business with the gun is too strong. It overwhelms everything else. Either cancel the gun or set the chase scene somewhere else. His friends witnessed it, but the neighbors didn't. I don't want it to interfere with the Anita scene. Or maybe it should be Lester who is chased.

But as is there can be comedy in his friends' reactions. Stevie, hero.

"I thought you was dead for sure!"

"That cop was nuts, man, really nuts!"

"Were you scared?"

Stevie playing tough guy: "Sure I was scared. Wouldn't you be?"

His running away has saved Lester. "They almost had me there." They think he ran purposely to distract the cops. Lester thanking him. Stevie going along with it.

Then Lester: "Never thought you could run so fast."

His slowness is legendary among them. They laugh and his glory is punctured.

"He practices in the morning. I seen him"

"Yeah, he's really got those legs in shape."

"They're gonna put him in the Olympics!"

"From now on we call him Speedy Stevie."

Good stuff. Hate to lose it.

Back on Montgomery Street. It's colder now, and he shivers

under his light jacket. Goes into the candy store, looking for his friends, finds Anita there drinking a cherry soda. Something is bothering her but we don't know what. Bertie is pouring chocolate syrup from a gallon jug into a dispenser. The thick glug-glug-glug of it.

"Where's everybody?"

"Up in the schoolyard."

Willy sitting in the back as before, drinking what might be that same bitter cup of coffee.

S: I'll see you later.

Goes to the schoolyard.

His friends are playing ringalievio. Nice emblem of the whole. You leave home base, get caught, get freed again.

"One-two-three ringalievio!"

Tricky lighting here. Kids moving in and out of shadows. The point of the game is, if you get down low, crawl on the ground, you can't be seen. The enemy appears suddenly out of the darkness.

"Hey, it's Stevie!" "Our hero!"

Eventually Stevie joins the game.

Some kind of transition—maybe cut to Max—then back to the schoolyard and Spider is there.

Do I want to call him Spider?

Big, hulking, vaguely misshapen. A heavy beard but girlish mannerisms and a high-pitched voice, a lumpish androgyne, a hormonal mess. His performance, his degradation.

Why does his image stick?

His simpering desire to join the circle of boys. The way he came around asking to be our victim. The rumors that the Pigtowners did things to him. Establish all this.

"Hey, look, it's the spider."

"Hey, Spider, wanna play?"

"How about a little Nellie action, Spider?"

"Yeah, a little Nellie action, Spi!"

Voices, darkness, shadow. For a moment they speak as a group, live as a group. But it's temporary and fragile, a thing of the moment. Spider somehow brings them together. The sense that their bonds to each other will soon be shattered, the summer is ending, they're going off to different high schools, different friends. But avoid the implicit sentimentality. Make it almost a parody of all those movie images of lost youth.

The mood, the way boys egg each other on, borrowing their courage and thus their cruelty from a common source that disappears when they're alone. These are basically nice Jewish kids who live in fear of the stronger, seemingly wilder working-class Italians—not to mention the blacks. In some sense, then, Stevie's experience is the experience of them all. Shoot it so that at the start of the sequence he is very much one of them, part of the group. Only later does he re-emerge.

———

Hard to picture it. I can remember it happening, and the mess of feelings it aroused in me, but I can't remember how we made it happen. And the point here is that we did make it happen, we drove the poor bastard to his degradation. And we enjoyed it— more than enjoyed it—there was something primal and ecstatic in it. That's what the sequence must suggest.

The cruelty of it, the cruelty of the group to the scapegoat, but no single one of us was really cruel. Besides, it was only cruel in a way; in other ways it wasn't cruel at all. We might not have wanted to be Spider, but that doesn't mean necessarily that he didn't want to be.

How much choice did he have?

Were we his victims as much as he was ours?

The relation of Spider to the rest of us, the way his apartness made us part of each other. We have to see the circle of boys forming quite literally around him. The way our clapping and encouragement merged to egg him on. This is more than inciden-tal. Do it right, catch the mechanism that brings about the

77

"Nellie" scene, and somehow you'll have caught the formation of community, the origins of Montgomery Street itself, the way it draws itself together around an image of its darkest and ugliest fears.

But now I'm knocking on an open door.

———

The group. Stevie, Lester, maybe half a dozen others. They need to be characterized. Do it with casting and you end up with a bunch of types, some agent's version of Brooklyn boys. Again that problem: how much to retrieve from memory, how much to imagine? Am I trying merely to recreate what was or create something new? Both, of course, and somehow both at once. But I can't get beyond the simple fact that my motive in this thing is the desire to go back, see it all again. My nonsensical nostalgia. Stu, Fred, Gary, Howie, Georgie, Floyd, Irky—I can't shake loose of them, they've become a part of me.

———

The schoolyard, in the dimness of a distant lamppost light, the boys have gathered around Spider.

Lester: Let's go, Spider, a little Nellie action.

Others: Come on, Spi! Hey, baby, it's Nellie time! Be a pal, Spider!

Sp: No. I can't.

L: Why not?

Tight on Spider. He smiles spookily: Because tonight is the night of the night.

L: You do Nellie, Spider, or I'm going to beat the crap out of you.

Sp: No.

Tense moment. Four beats.

Then Lester smiles meanly.

L: Okay, then get the hell out of the schoolyard. We don't want you here.

Others: Yeah, get out of here. Go on. Vanish!

Sp (upset): I don't have to go.

Get the hell out of here!

Sp (whimpering): It's a free country.

Get out of here! Beat it! Get lost!

They menace him. One of them gives him a shove.

His point of view, scanning their faces. Stevie looks just a little embarrassed. Then close on Spider. Something tightens in his face.

Sp: Wait, wait. I'll do it. (Then with more dignity) But I have to get paid, you know. You always have to pay for a show.

L: How much?

Sp: One dime each.

Stevie: Aw, the hell with him. Come on, let's play.

L: Here's the deal. You do the show. If we like it, then we pay you.

Sp: No, no. That's not the way I do business.

Stevie: Come on, the hell with him.

Spider looks at Stevie, in some way singling him out, as though there were some hidden bond between them.

Others: Come on, let's have a little Nellie action! Let's go, Spider! We want Nellie, we want Nellie! Do it, baby!

Sp: Okay, okay, don't rush me. I need to get myself ready, you know. You have to work up to it, you know. You can't just do it, you know.

He walks a few steps away from them, over to the wall (NO BALL PLAYING . . .). The boys exchange smiles, pokes in the ribs. The camera passes through this, closing in on Spider as he does a few awkward knee bends, cracks his knuckles, mutters to himself, all the while undergoing some sort of transformation. His face is to the wall. He moans softly. Then he leaps up into the air, swinging his long arms monkeyishly, and half-lopes, half-dances back toward the camera, his fervent face filling the screen.

Another angle. Looking down on the circle of boys gathering around Spider. He makes obscene noises. Then, with lewd slow menace, he chants:

> The clock strikes one
> The fun's begun
> Nellie put your belly next to mine.

He claps hands, starting a primitive rhythm which the boys pick up. He whirls around doing his dance, leaping, lowering himself toward the ground, leaping up again. The camera dollies in slowly on this. Then tight on his face, the long obscene jaw, the transfixed eyes.

> The clock strikes two
> She's on my shoe—woo—woo
> Nellie
> Put your belly
> Oh next to mine!

He's a grotesque parody of some unknown ape, a manic contortionist, twisting and leaping, but he's caught them up in it. The mood subtly changes as the performance draws them in. They mutter words of encouragement, clap harder. One or two of them even start to sing along with him. Others start laughing, but the laughter eventually goes out of control, verges on a kind of hysteria.

> The clock strikes three
> She's on my knee . . .

> The clock strikes four
> I've got her on the floor . . .

He has managed to conjure up for them an invisible but very palpable Nellie. He leans over her, rubbing his thighs, caresses her—the mime here must be good—leaps up again, and some of the boys don't follow him with their eyes because they're looking at her!

And Stevie?

At first he's been as caught up in it as the others, caught in Spider's web; but then, somehow, it's lost to him, he to it. He stops looking at Spider and (the spell is broken) he starts looking at the others, to see how they're reacting. He's disturbed by it all, but he's not sure why. He thinks it's because he's disgusted, that they're doing something wrong. This remains in the background.

On Spider. Bumps and grinds. The dance ever more lewd, the boys ever more enmeshed. The hand-clapping begins to approximate a heartbeat, maybe even a heartbeat on the sound track. The clock-heart that must tick-beat in every art, even this. Faster, louder, faster and louder.

> The clock strikes five
> She's come alive
> Nellie
> Please please please put your pink belly
> Oh, oh, oh, oh
> Next to mine!

Murmurs from the group: Yeah, oh yeah! Do it, Spider! Come on, come on!

Some of them, embarrassed by their arousal, are giggling. Lester beams happily; he's the impresario, he's arranged it all.

On Stevie: what's he thinking about? The rabbi's wife, the morning shame. Maybe a flicker of her, subliminal, two or three frames. Nellie has, in a sense, become *too* real for him, and that's what breaks the illusion. Now he's torn. He wants to go, get away from it, but going will lead to later teasing, the boys shaming him. His indecision. His brow all furrows, a sense of growing hardness in his face.

> The clock strikes sex
> We're up to our necks
> Oh Nellie
> Sweet sweet Nellie
> Oh Nellie
> Put that belly
> Closer, closer, closer to mine!

Spider's face, twisted and sweating. Stevie's face. The circle from above. Lester. Spider. Stevie.

Then, frightened by his boldness, feeling both brave and cowardly, confused and very determined, Stevie simply turns his back on the scene and walks away.

The circle closes quickly around the space he's left. The performance continues.

> The clock strikes seven
> We're flying to heaven . . .

Fading in the background as Stevie plods slowly, hot-faced, down the schoolyard steps.

———

Is it really so obvious? The door seems open, but try to walk through it and you're likely to bump your nose. The essence of Spider, the reason he becomes attractive in some perverse way— and the thing has to be done so that he does become attractive, transcends his pathetic geekiness—is that, in a sense, he's free. By being rejected and despised he's been liberated. That's why he's not afraid to dredge up Nellie out of his own inner darkness, create her out of his agony for all to see. He's not really a scapegoat and victim, or not merely that. His grotesque performance recapitulates the birth of community because it is the image of the freedom we fled. He is a primeval bard singing to savages of their own savageness, and in his mirror a new world is made.

Don't forget, though, that the circle is exclusively masculine.

Also, the kid suffers for it. Not while he's performing—that's bliss—but later on, by himself, having to live with himself, he really suffers.

We don't want to be him.

———

Next, why does Stevie walk away? Is it credible? I didn't. There seems to be a hole in the middle of it. I'm getting too far into this thing now, a bit obsessed. Do what seems right. You never really know what you've done until you see the rushes. Besides, the question of whether he's the sort of character who would walk away is irrelevant. Remember: no such thing as character. The fact that he walks away makes him what he is. Action defines. What I ought to do is get a crew together, plunge in, and improvise. Damn this passion to foresee and control! To film only what I have plotted and planned. My literary bias, the heritage of words. The stiffness at the core of *Centerpiece*, as though I were afraid the damn thing would explode. The way I always seem to be scrabbling to avoid disaster. Getting worse as I get older, too, my fear of the accidental, the aleatory. Is that why I'm afraid of using her? That she'll steal my show? That I won't be able to contain her vitality? The protective armor of Montgomery Street bred in me. But the worth of the thing will come through how it's done, not through what I think of it. If the point is leaping, maybe you have to leap to show it. Max's problem: relent for a moment and chaos comes.

———

More and more I'm fabricating instead of remembering, working, trying to squeeze a few last drops from a well that's run dry. Did I think I would be inspired forever? Leave, go back to N.Y.? Go take a walk on whatever remains of Montgomery Street? I've exhausted Sète. Another day or two, try to finish Stevie, then I'll go.

———

The Anita scene, a resolution of Stevie's fantasies, a whiff of the simple realities of empathy, affection. He mistakes it for love. He's taken in because he doesn't have to be Captain Marvel to woo her. He doesn't even set out to woo her; he's just being friendly. Earthbound, no big passion, just a boy and a girl groping toward each other. He comes down out of the schoolyard, alone and prickly, and there she is. And she's been there all the time. It's just that he had to surrender some portion of his ambitions and fantasies before he could see her.

She's not pretty. There's a taint of acridity about her, damp circles in her blouse beneath her arms, a miasma of rough complexion, and somewhere in the background a rigid—why not say frigid—mother who burdens her with household chores.

Max tells someone: "You wanna know how a girl will turn out, look at her mother."

She's leaning against a car (that new car with a bashed fender?) in front of 480. A dozen garbage cans line the street waiting for the morning pickup. The lights in the candy store blink off. The *yentehs* are folding up their chairs and creeping off to bed. A siren in the distance.

"Whacha doin'?"

"Nothin'."

She's chewing the skin around her fingernails. Stevie sees her mother hanging out of the second-story window above, obviously looking for someone.

What are they going to talk about?

Is this the scene I want? Have I prepared for it? Is this where Stevie's been heading?

The way things are there even when you haven't bothered to notice them. Don't establish her, setting her up. Play down those meetings when he's delivering groceries and coming up to the schoolyard. She has existed up to this point simply as part of the background, so familiar that her coming to the center of Stevie's attention makes her wondrous and new. There comes that shock of recognition, Stevie's life rearranging itself so that for a few moments, maybe a few days, she enters the foreground of his thoughts, ultimately to recede again. Nothing more, a kind of throwaway scene—and yet it is also climactic.

Subliminal possibilities. We record more than we know we see. The way external events derive their importance by matching inner patterns of experience, our internal sense of form, the order of our lives. Which isn't how it's usually done, the way I learned to do it, composing images so that what's important is what draws the eye. The tyranny of plot and manipulation. Free the audience. Suddenly Anita is there! But a style that throws away the conventions of narrative will be disturbing. Fail to establish Anita early on and she'll seem an afterthought, a disruption of form. Disturbing because it's too real. Depict randomness by means of randomness and you end up with a mess. You have to have it both ways at once. Anita has been there throughout, we just haven't been forced to notice her. When the scene comes we are surprised, perhaps even disturbed: Who's she? Have we seen her before? Then ultimately there comes the satisfaction of realizing that she has, in fact, been prepared for, that the scene is obligatory, we just haven't remembered previous images vividly enough. That's the style, and that will be the pleasure of it, shaking them out of their easy manipulated responses, like the first shooting in *Bonnie and Clyde,* or the way Hitchcock killed off Janet Leigh just as we had settled down to spend the whole picture with her. Anyway, something akin to that.

———

He comes down out of the schoolyard, sees her, is going to pass her by, but the way she looks at him, not quite beckoning, and his own momentary turmoil, draw him over to her. Her mother at the window, her nervousness: something's wrong. At first Stevie doesn't quite take it in.

What the hell are they going to talk about?

85

The Nellie song, the noise of the boys in the background.

"What are they doing up there?"

"Spider's putting on a show."

"He's such a pathetic creep. Why don't they just leave him alone?"

Stevie shrugs.

"How come you came down?"

Pause.

Finally, Stevie: How about if we walk around to Carvel?

A: I'll have to ask the boss.

Medium shot. She takes a few steps away from him, calls to her mother: Stevie and I are gonna walk around to Carvel.

Tight on mother, her worried meanness: No you're not. You're coming up in a minute.

A: We'll be right back.

Mother: I said I want you to stay here.

A (turning to Stevie, under her breath, mimicking): I said I want you to stay here. Witch!

A loud burst of laughter and shouting from the schoolyard.

A: Ooh, I hate that woman!

S: I think—

A: What?

S: Nothing.

A: Tell me.

S: It's nothing.

A: Come on. It's not nothing. What were you going to say?

S (with unexpected boldness): I was going to say we should go anyway.

A (liking the idea): God, I wish I could.

S: Well, come on then. Let's go.

A (playing with thoughts of rebellion): She'd kill me.

S: She's not going to kill you.

A (nervous laugh): I can't.

S (more brazen than he's ever been): Sure you can.

On her, on him. Their faces glow with anticipation. But before it can be decided there comes the sound of distant singing.

On Anita: she stiffens and loses interest in everything but that singing. Panic on her face. Stevie doesn't know at first what's going on. The singing gets louder. Then Anita's mother, in a huge rush, comes out of the apartment house, passes them by. She's wearing a raincoat thrown over a housedress; her feet are slippered, a glimpse of fluffy pale pink things flopping against the sidewalk. She heads toward the corner.

S: Something's—

He makes as if to follow her.

Anita grabs his hand, whispers urgently: Stay right here.

S: But—

A: I said stay here!

Something of her mother's imperiousness has crept into her tone. She grips his hand, leads him further into the shadows.

Stevie's point of view: we see her mother plunging along the street, her father emerging from around the corner, obviously quite drunk, singing:

> Stop rambling, stop gambling
> Stop staying out late at night
> Stay home with your wife and your family
> Stay there by the fireside bright—
>
> Irene, good ni-i-ight . . .

He's a slender, handsome man who seems younger than his wife. Boyish. The sort of guy who will go up to the schoolyard for a catch with the boys, buy them sodas, slap their behinds. We'll have seen him going off to work early in the morning, and have mistaken his glee at leaving his house for chipperness. Maybe give him a scene with Max.

That he should come home drunk astonishes Stevie. For Anita, of course, the scene is familiar enough.

87

Tight on Stevie and Anita practically huddling together.

S: But that's—

A: Sshh!

Her hand squeezing his, her knuckles pressed white.

Long shot of her parents.

He comes toward his wife slowly, staggering a bit, still singing. She rushes to meet him. The song breaks. We can just about make out their conversation.

Her: Must everyone hear you!

Him: Hi.

Her: God damn you, you be quiet or so help me I'll—

Him: I had to work late.

The fierceness and strength of her anger. She takes him by the arm, practically drags him along the street as though he were a naughty child.

Reaction shot: Stevie and Anita watching, not wanting to watch. Anita fighting back tears, chewing her lip. Still gripping Stevie's hand.

Her parents, closer and closer.

Him: Then Hymie and I stopped off for a beer.

Her: You just get yourself upstairs.

He is thoroughly cowed.

They go by Stevie and Anita, paying no attention to them, then their backs as they enter the building.

Him: You don't have to—

Her: I said keep quiet!

Somehow the feeling is that when she gets him upstairs she's going to spank him.

Only after they're gone does Anita burst into tears. Stevie is helpless. His boldness of a few moments earlier has quite vanished, but he thinks to put an awkward arm around her, and she allows herself to sob for a moment on his shoulder.

The sobbing abruptly ends. She has her mother's hardness in her.

S: What can I do?

Stevie the innocent. For him drunkenness is a *goyische* affliction, red-eyed Irishmen emerging from the Shamrock Inn on Nostrand Avenue, or those filthy gray men in filthy gray overcoats he's seen on the subway or sleeping in doorways in Manhattan.

S: What can I do?

There had to be in it the hurt acceptance of responsibility along with a childish plaint of bewilderment.

She just shakes her head.

S: Does it happen often?

Again she shakes her head, struggling to hold on to herself. Her lower lip quivering.

The fact is her father is no alcoholic; he simply gets drunk once in a while. There is nothing terribly sordid in it; it merely seems sordid by the standards of Montgomery Street. The tone has to balance both of these.

"I never knew."

Ambiguous. Is he finding out something lots of others have known about, or has he stumbled onto one of the street's closely guarded secrets? Has he discovered the obvious or the arcane? What a maddening place it was! I never did find out. Is Stevie especially naïve or is naïveté the general truth of the place? Has to be both.

Anita finally pulls herself together. With her mother's fierceness: "You have to promise me you'll never tell anyone."

S: Of course I won't.

A: Promise!

S: Cross my heart and hope to die.

He makes the heart-crossing gesture with just the right balance of childish seriousness and grown-up irony. She reacts with childish solemnity and grown-up suspicion. He tries to smile away her suspicions.

She snuffles up gook into her nose. The crying has reddened her face and she seems quite ugly, but Stevie finds something exquisite in her ugliness, is drawn to her, her hurt, her need, her vulnerability. He's loving being heroic.

There comes over his face an echo of the look he gave the rabbi's wife.

Not clear how this plays itself out.

A: I hate her! God, how I hate her!

He has to make some kind of gesture.

A reaching.

He thinks somehow that he has to appease her.

He pulls out of his pocket a package of Life Savers. Several of them are gone and the tube of paper is neatly folded down.

We will have seen him purchase those Life Savers in the morning, and eat them one at a time at crucial moments during the day.

He was sucking a Life Saver while waiting for Lester in Chinatown; popped one into his mouth when the subway got stuck; etc.

Yellow, green, red, orange.

S: Want a Life Saver?

A: Got a red one?

S: I like the green.

He'll eat the last Life Saver when he undresses for bed. An orange one.

What else does he carry in his pockets? Coins, the Life Savers, a dirty handkerchief, a compass, a pack of matches, a little pair of dogs, black and white, with magnets on the bottom. A bit of stone crystal. A wallet. A comb. Three firecrackers.

A: I like the peppermint ones the best.

S: I hate them.

Pause.

S: I don't know what to say.

A: You don't have to say anything.

S (blundering a bit): I like your father.

A: It's her.

Pause.

A: I dread going up there. I just dread it.

Stevie is about to say something, but then rather boisterously the boys are coming down out of the schoolyard. Before they're seen, with a kind of instant understanding, Stevie and Anita go down the steps that lead to the cellar.

Corny?

The hell with it. They're fourteen years old. All they're going to do is give each other a puppyish kiss—though with all the throb and tension and swelling sound track of the Big Love Scene in a thousand maudlin movies.

And they've gotten just about that far when—again play with the cliché—her mother sticks her head out of the window above: Neee-ter! Get up here!

Anita pops her head out of the opening: Coming!

Mother: What are you doing down there?

A: Looking for something.

She signals Stevie to stay in hiding and goes.

He counts to thirty, mouthing the numbers, and comes out. Goes down Montgomery Street, ignoring the boys across the street.

A falsetto voice behind his back: Night night, Stevie!

Goes through the glass door of his building.

Meets his father coming downstairs.

Scene with his father? I've side-stepped that problem. Hard to do them together. Same with Max and his wife. There's a connection here. Women shaming men. The matriarchy of Montgomery Street. The men provide, the women live. Which must be why life felt so thin there, so dull, so drab, why only the prism of memory can make it shine. The best poor Benny could do was become an anomaly, a Jewish drunk. Note the connection between him and Bono, in so many ways the same, and yet so different. A couple of boys. The way Michelle drifted later on toward that Pigtown thug. Because the boys of Montgomery Street, like their fathers, must have seemed to her to lack some essential seriousness. Which is why I hated it there. And I haven't

91

quite dealt with it even now. In a sense I've only been diddling, tiptoeing around the truth of the place. Bertie Grossman, sure, but she's only a hint, and Anita's mother is only an echo. Stevie with his parents. They weren't shrews on Montgomery Street, strong-willed and fierce. They didn't have to be. All they had to do was be mothers. I can't conceive Max's wife without conceiving Max's shame. The game I learned to play. Is that what I'm afraid of?

They would struggle on Montgomery Street, the husbands and wives, but no matter how it appeared, the men would never win.

Portnoy's cliché.

Curious though. It wasn't being Jewish. The Italians never seemed shamed by their women, but then neither did the *Hasidim*. When Stevie's with the rabbi's wife he's really terrified, he cowers—and that's something she can't understand, she never sees it because in her world the men use her or ignore her or rely on her as they, the men, please. Stevie fails as a supplicant, but he might have succeeded as a brute.

Can that be what I want in Max? Is that his uniqueness?

Stevie fled not from Spider's degradation, but from the all-too-real image of Nellie.

Same reason I came to Sète, isn't it? And why lately I've been feeling so fidgety here.

Damn them! Damn them! They just can't leave us alone!

———

Keep it brief and simple, a tag end to the Anita scene.

He runs into his father on the stairs.

Father: Your mother sent me to look for you. You know what time it is?

It's a kind of family ritual, one of the great embarrassments of Stevie's life, his father, a figure of fun, tramping grimly along Montgomery Street to fetch him home.

"Your mother sent me out to look for you."

S: So here I am.

92

F (inspecting him): What's the matter?

S: Nothing.

F: You're all red in the face.

S: I was playing.

No real contact. There never will be.

He turns and heads upstairs, Stevie following, staring at the old man's big slablike back.

Cut to Max?

———

Stevie's mother, maybe in the morning: "Whatsa matter with you. You got ants in the pants?"

———

The fidgets, restlessness, the itch of the familiar. How the line of your life goes stale. The "rut." "Wheels, we gotta get some wheels." Max holding that gun realizes that everything has become new.

———

Talked to Z. He wants me in London right away. Needs me is what he said. Important business to discuss. When can I be there? And like a good little boy I told him I'd come, I was sick of Sète anyway, I'd fly in from Marseilles tomorrow. It doesn't matter. Summer's ending. Incredible how the town is emptying out now that August is over. The French seem to go on holiday in lock step. The place has taken on the air of the fish market after all the trucks have left and the boats have gone to berth, and all that remains is the sea stench and wet pavement. So let it be London. J's still there, and she seems to hold the key to Max, and thus to the project. I can't do him without knowing her. Besides, Z said Mort has sent him a packet for me. The researcher's report, I suppose. So he knew I'd be going. I sit here imagining I'm free, and meanwhile they're making plans for me. What a rhyme. Poet and he don't know it.

What do they want from me?

I'll know soon enough.

———

Stevie preparing for bed, in his underwear (refuses to wear pajamas), sucking that last Life Saver, a big stupid smile on his face as he thinks of Anita. Play it for laughs. He takes his pillow, embraces it, dances it around. Then he seems to realize the direness of his entanglement, his entrapment. What the hell is he going to say to her tomorrow? He frowns, scowls, looks around the room, its memories; becomes aware that he's giving it all up. That wasn't what he had in mind!

His mother's voice: "Nu, Stevie, you going to sleep?"

"Yeah, yeah, in a minute."

Goes to the table, picks up that unfinished wing, rubs his finger along the smooth balsa wood, soothing himself. Trims a little rough spot with an X-Acto knife, examines it, rubs it with a bit of sandpaper. Then for a moment he's at play, imagining the finished plane flying; then he imagines himself flying. A note of momentary regression before he goes to bed. The quietest possible ending. Unless we end with Max.

Not quite, but it will have to do for now.

Max. His antiques. Buying and selling. His wife. What sort of marriage? A mistress for him? A lover for her? Brooding: what's happened to him, he used to be so ambitious! Chewing a big cigar. The wet gnawed disgusting end of it. But what is he going to *do*? He finds the gun. The pressures have been mounting on him. Have him go berserk? Shooting up Montgomery Street, shot down in the end by the cops. Or have some other character (Bono?) do the shooting. He kills Max, or maybe just wounds him. A scene in a hospital.

Dreck!

Maybe I don't need Max, do just Stevie, have everything revolve around him. I have enough material. There's enough texture there. A growing-up movie, *Bildungscinema*. Like a dozen flops I can think of.

In the course of that day Max—

Have Max murder Stevie?

Violence is the product of a failed imagination, as much in movies as in life.

Mort called. Strange conversation. He seemed to be setting me up for something. Made sure to mention that the advance bookings for *Centerpiece* have been "a little disappointing." The Cannes prize means something in Paris, and maybe in New York, but it doesn't sell tickets in Topeka or Moline. The weather back home is glorious. He ran into Peter on Ninth Avenue. Peter sends his regards. Have a good time in London.

Max must be made bold, large, colorful. He must be alive with energy, a talker, a joker. A man who plays and in playing disturbs the drabness and solemnity around him. He must be comic, earthy. The swelled and broken pavement, earth pushing through. Earth aspiring to sky.

A scene in the synagogue: he gets a whiff of religion. A scene in the police station. A young girl sitting there wrapped in a man's huge raincoat. What happened to her? We see him going about his business, fixing things, selling things, buying up some old furniture. The gun. His wife. Their marriage in crisis. But their marriage has been in crisis for years. The way you go along with it because you're stuck. Until something comes along to unstick you. Max coming unstuck? A mistress? Is J going to be the mistress or the wife?

The space between waking and dreams, the opening through which we plunge each night, that dreadful transition. Going to bed is an act of faith. Why do I always have so much trouble sleeping the night before a day of travel?

———

My adrenaline's up. I'm ready for a fight, but I don't know yet what the weapons will be or over what territory the battle will take place. I'm not even sure we've chosen up sides. But that there will be a battle is certain. Mort made that clear enough. And I suspect the implication was that I was going to be whipped into line for my own good. It was really a strange conversation. "All you've got is a foot in the door," he said. "You'll have to shove a bit to go on through." Meaning I should do what Z wants me to do? That there'll be time for independence later on? That I'm still only "promising" and that my career is in Z's hands? Or am I supposed to buck him?

———

I always take my judgment from a Fool
Because his judgment is so very Cool,
Not prejudic'd by feelings great or small.
Amiable state! he cannot feel at all.

———

Called Mort back and we had a heart-to-heart. He pooh-poohed everything, suggested that too much isolation was making me paranoid. I have to trust him, I guess. The premise is that he's working for me. But he has a lawyer's mind and his instincts are thoroughly commercial. Z's tastes are unreliable, but the damn thing about Mort is he has no taste at all. He's thoroughly a pragmatist, which is to say a cynic. I suppose I'm a kind of cynic, too, but of the opposite, the romantic variety. I kick against my own illusions. There, that's Max, isn't it?

Max, Max, Max.

We see in the mirror just what we want to see.

If I don't do my movie now, if I don't control it, I'll end up hacking forever, being nothing at all.

———

J met me at Heathrow with a hug and a kiss, and apologies from

96

Z, who was all tied up with Lord Somebody of the BBC. The flight was bizarre. Cops with burp guns at the Marseilles airport. An hour and a half delay. An Arab gentleman out of a John Huston movie sharing my seat. He insisted on conversation, and so we settled the Middle East conflict between us. Did I know that the British once planned to set up a Jewish state in Uganda? The crazy fact is, I did. Israel, after all, was the Valhalla of Montgomery Street, and there's very little I didn't learn about it. Together we regretted the Irgun. We agreed there must be an end to violence. Are we not, Arab and Jew, brothers in our Semitism? Do we not share a plague of noses? Eventually we came down over an unexpected English countryside, all burned brown by the drought, parched and tawny in the glare of sun. London at first glance seems a troubled city, gray-faced, grim. J said she doesn't like it here. She wants to go home. Where's that? If only she knew.

That gave us a topic of conversation for the drive into town. We shared our mutual sense of homelessness. Was she merely being empathetic or does it really bother her as much as it does me? I admitted to being twice dispossessed. I heard myself saying I only feel at home in the movies. She asked about my wife, my children. We worked at being witty and sophisticated, a couple of kids, Brooklyn and Queens, trying not to show off their tingling nerve ends, our sense of awe ("Gee, we're really in London!"), our fear of the big wide unfamiliar world.

I asked her finally, had to ask her, how it was, her connection to Z.

"It's all contractual," she said. "He owes me a role."

Z, by the way, has insisted on paying for my room at the Dorchester. "It's where all the rich London Jews have their kids *bar-mitzvahed*." I almost demurred, but I decided I might as well start the game on his board, give him the illusion of advantage.

Thirty pounds a day he's paying for this room.

Fanciest doorknobs I've ever seen.

We sat in the lobby and waited for Z, both of us in jeans, looking so scruffy and out of place that everyone knew we were crazy show-biz Americans. The British are stingy with ice but not with tonic. To entertain me—if we are going to go any further she will have to learn not to entertain me—she told me the long sad story of her life.

No big surprises. Girlhood in Forest Hills, teen-age bohemianism at the High School of Music and Art, a couple of stoned years at Wellesley, the artsy theater-major type, all Hesse and hugs and whole wheat bread. Then off off Broadway ("baring my boobs") and an abortion and a few nasty months of marriage to a playwright who wanted to set up a *ménage à trois*, bring his boyfriend home. Recuperation in California. Bit parts on Broadway. Television commercials—girl on tiger-skin rug peddling cologne. First victim of the homicidal rapist in half a dozen copshow teasers. She does, in fact, have some of that vulnerable culpability rapists and TV directors look for. An apartment in the East Eighties, not far from my own, my refuge from E, my nightmare maze of rooms. The Method. A long tedious affair with a *Newsweek* book critic with fancy tastes. And finally her Big Break, a fat role as a good-natured whore, brilliantly enacted, in a movie that Z, for obscure tax reasons, refuses to release. Which is presumably why he owes her, why he's been so hot to palm her off on me.

Then it was the three of us, after a big hearty welcome, off to dinner at Simpson's, Z's idea of very British, no shoptalk allowed.

Z as father image, a side of him he's never shown me before. By the third bottle of wine he was damply sentimental, put his arms around the both of us and declared that I was his pride and she was his joy. We drank to hope. Hope for what? Not clear.

What do I signify for them? What do they want from me? I feel like I'm being tried, but I don't know for what or what's at stake. Have they conspired or am I being paranoid? And if

they've conspired, if they expect to drag me kicking and screaming into something, what will that something be? Something I
may just have wanted for myself anyway? Who knows? That
could be the case.

Anyway, my heart was thumping like a schoolboy's stupid
heart as I sat there between them, as though only my presence
connected them, as though—why not say it?—the three of us
were parts of some larger scheme. Clammy feeling, that. Everything comes in threes. Somehow in it all came the notion that Z
might want me to convince him as much as he wants to convince
me. That he was hoping I would see through his bluster, buck
him. The way he keeps saying: "What do I know?" The tension
between us may still prove creative.

Met this morning with Z, just the two of us *tête-à-tête*. I was
supposed to be impressed, and was, by the opulence of his suite,
the big English breakfast for two being delivered on a roll cart,
the toast still warm under a pink linen cozy, eggs and bacon and
sausages and grilled tomatoes shimmering beneath a silvery
dome. He likes it here in London, I suppose, because he is
reminded of the elegance of old movies, *Room Service, Dinner at
Eight, Grand Hotel*, some adolescent vision, the richness of
privilege we've lost. I let him do the talking. He was in an elegiac
mood, or perhaps let himself wax reminiscent as part of some
larger, harder strategy.

I heard all about growing up Jewish in the thirties in
Philadelphia, city of brotherly love and gentlemen's agreements.
I heard about his adventures as a field lieutenant during the war,
how he killed just one German, and how he was one of the first
Americans to see Buchenwald. I heard about his marriage and
how he regretted never having kids. Is he impotent, sterile—or
was it her fault? Maybe Mort knows; have to ask. I began to
suspect that he wanted me to do a film of his life, that he was
presenting a scenario, "The Demitycoon," but no, it's only that

without quite realizing it, he has learned to see his life in cinematic terms. A Dmitri Tiomkin sound track plays behind his memories. And all he seemed to be trying to do, poor fumbling fellow (or cool pro), was to express what he eventually confessed was a fondness for me.

I'm not sure he actually knows himself whether he was conning me or being sincere. Or if it matters. The articulation may be pure Hollywood hokum, but the feeling behind it may be heartfelt nonetheless. He called me his hope for salvation. He implied that nursing my genius would somehow justify his money-tainted soul. He painted a rainbow future in which he would produce the "authentic" films I would make. And what, for him, is an "authentic" film? A film with "heart and truth" in it; a film that won't leave him feeling cheap and queasy; a film that is not merely a commercial success; a film he can dote upon in his old age the way he might a bright and handsome grandson. A film that is more than a funhouse mirror, I wanted to add, but didn't.

Which is why he's allowed me so much freedom so far, why he's waited so patiently for a treatment from me.

And then, of course, the but. He has received from an editor pal of his the pull sheets of a soon-to-be-published novel called *The Olisbos*. It's bold, it's brilliant, it's magical, it's dynamic, it catches something crucial about the way we live our lives—in short he believes I can make it into a truly marvelous movie. Will I consent to read it?

What choice do I have?

———

I'm falling into something here I don't understand. Z is successful because you can't separate his sincerity from his caginess. I suspect, really, it's not the book he's concerned with, but me, my reaction to it. Which is why this is so important to him. He's already phoned up to see if I've started it yet. The game we're in—and I still don't know the rules.

So I've read it, or enough of it. It's trivial stuff, though I suppose from another point of view it's no more trivial than *Montgomery Street*. Tough woman photographer takes as lover neurotic classical actor. Slick and funny. I can see why Z thought I'd like it; it's a kind of counterpart to *Centerpiece*. Ironically romantic; beautiful people moving through a gorgeous world; lots of darkrooms and long lenses; sex play. A book just clever enough and bad enough to make a decent movie. Conceivably commercial, especially if it hits the best-seller lists—but hardly the balm for the soul that Z was talking about. No, I can't believe he really admires it, or thought I would. Or does he? Do I have him all wrong? Can it be that, at bottom, he's a simp?

"It seemed to Sara then that the very worst thing in the world was to die. Not simply because of her instinctive fear of oblivion, but because death would thwart her curiosity. The world unreels in time like a wonderful movie and she just had to see what would happen next. But she also knew that to live was not just a matter of sitting in a theater. No, life was also like those still shots from movies they hang in glass cases, tantalizing, frustrating, inviting you into the dark."

Not a good night. Too much on my mind. Hectic dreams, quickly repressed. One glimpse remains. I was trying to fold a big piece of thin-sliced buttered bread into an envelope so I could mail it to someone. Who? Don't know. Probably an Andalusian dog.

Begged off seeing Z. Told him I wanted to reread the thing. Need some more time to plan my response.

Connived to spend the afternoon with J. We browsed in Harrods (Keats reminded Yeats of a little boy with his nose pressed flat against the sweet-shop window) and then went to Madame

Tussaud's. She loved it; I figured she would. And yet she claims to believe in spontaneity, nature, passion. She has read with great enthusiasm the works of Wilhelm Reich. She has sat naked in a thermal bath at the Esalen Institute. She made it clear she was available—and the damn thing is, through all those years of being overfed by E, she was exactly the kind of alternative I had in mind. But business first. I asked if she had read *The Olisbos*. I was not altogether surprised to learn she had never heard of it. We talked movies. She identifies with the girl in *La Strada*. She can't abide Bergman. She believes Renoir *fils* is a greater artist than Renoir *père*. She works very hard at being complicated. She is spending the evening with a cousin who works for an oil company, and so we have put off an uncomfortable scene.

I'm seeing Z in the morning.

And so to bed.

———

A nightsweat; then a plunge into sleep that was as drab and dark as a tunnel; then I woke up aching and fogged as though I had been drugged. Can't face the thought of washing my face. My tongue is as dry and hard as pavement. My teeth hurt, as though I was clenching them all night.

What am I going to tell him? I won't know until I actually hear myself saying it. The nagging thought that I could do that book, make something good of it. The feeling that Montgomery Street is simply too drab. What was it I was thinking about—the memory I woke up with: yes, that time my father tried to hit me and I grabbed his hand. It must have happened when I was just about Stevie's age, just coming into adult strength. Give him that scene: they have a fight about something and his father tries to hit him and he stops him, matching strength against strength, will against will. How, having beaten the man, he runs out of the house and walks around for a while in the heat waiting for the sky to fall, God to chastise him for dishonoring his father. It was the bitterest of all possible triumphs, and I suppose some part of my diffidence with Z stems from it. And I can't even remember what the fight was about!

How strong do I dare be with him? How strong, really, does he want me to be?

Stevie and Max together? The way every man, in a sense, becomes your father?

Odd, how distant the whole thing has become, how I've stopped thinking about it since I came to London, as though I were afraid to go on without his permission. But it's not permission I need, it's money. Why struggle with it if it will never be filmed?

Stevie and his father. I don't want to do that scene, but it has to be implied. How you have to defeat him to be free. The destruction of fathers—unless, of course, they choose to live in us.

Indecisive meeting, desultory. Z was jovial. He said he didn't want to rush me into a decision, that he was sure in the end we'd see eye to eye. Showed me some audience-reaction samples from *Centerpiece*. The wit leaves some behind. The sex scenes may not be erotic enough (of course not, the dopes). They fed all this crap into their computer and predicted an "optimal" gross of ten million. Maybe it could go higher if the promotional budget is raised, but not so high it would be worth raising it. Then Z promised to raise it anyway. He's willing to break even, maybe even take a loss. Talked in terms of a long-range investment in me. I suppose the idea is to bind me so closely to him that I won't go off at some future time and be my own producer. How much of this comes from Mort? Mort sits in New York and takes care of my interests, but what in God's name does he suppose my interests to be?

It's my own doing. I wanted to be free to make movies without worrying about the business end of it, but if you don't take the business in hand, if you don't control it, you're not free at all. Maybe I should go back to hacking out scripts, spin my dreams on paper, do the playful part, let someone else do the work of production. Never grow up.

I want it both ways at once. So I'd better get used to the tension.

———

It was the bitterest of all possible triumphs because it was too easy, because it proved my father's weakness, not my strength. They didn't give us enough to struggle against, the men of Montgomery Street, because their women had already unmanned them. And so we took up the illusion of our own manhood, through the hollow rituals of *bar mitzvahs* and schooling and adolescent sex. But a man does not become a man in relation to women, only in relation to other men. He must prove himself in that world first, and that's what I've sought to film. Which is why I've resisted using J. She clouds the issue, just as she's clouding the issue here, now, between Zuckerman and me. Should she vanish, our struggle would go on, maybe even intensify, because the energy of it would no longer dribble away in secondary considerations.

Make it clear that Stevie's crucial problems are the ones he has with Lester, with those comic hoodlums, with Korski, Benny, his father; that the rabbi's wife, Anita, his mother are merely diversions.

I suppose I never forgave E for giving me only daughters.

The battle between the sexes is comedy; the struggle within the sexes is tragedy.

Zuckerman.

My wretched desire to please him, be his fair-haired boy.

Does he want me to do what he says he wants me to do, or does he expect, thus want me, to thwart him?

Toby Zuckerman.

Zuckerman Zuckerman Zuckerman

TZ

Damn him! Damn the cagy game he's playing!

Sleepless. Getting almost as bad as last year. Tension; creative, I hope. Relax the mind, let thoughts come as they will, things start going in circles.

Style is the visible manifestation of the underlying reality of a thing. To apprehend the meaning of style, one must understand the relationship between surface (appearance) and depth (actuality). Bad style, which is to say false style, is a conflict between appearance and actuality—as in West's description of Hollywood houses in *Day of the Locust*.

Fair enough.

Next. The appreciation, even the creation of authentic style in any object (say a movie) is analogous to the uses of empathy in human relationships. Empathy, on which all community finally depends, is the understanding of the being behind the behavior, the clothes, the haircut, the image, the clutter of day-to-day acts.

Z says one thing but I suspect he wants me to *see* something else. We all do that.

The ruined life like the ruined style is a discontinuity between surface and depth. When Stevie dons a riveted belt, slicks back his hair, apes his notion of toughness, he's heading for disaster. When he walks away from Spider's show, he is being merely and simply and luckily himself.

Most films manipulate feeling by manipulating the responses of the audience to surfaces—violence, sight gags, scenery. I hate it when they come out of a theater stunned to silence, still caught in their lonely dream chambers. Create empathy and they will leave the theater chatting happily, alive to each other.

Aesthetic appreciation, or perhaps aesthetic discrimination, is thus analogous to and perhaps follows from empathy.

Homer singing the journey of Ulysses created around himself the civilization of Greece.

A hermit cannot enter a work of art. It is for him a mere

105

mirror and he bumps his nose against the ugly image of himself. Don't let yourself be that hermit.

Like the person who can judge a melon by thumping the rind with a fingernail. (Let Korski sell fruit?) Connects to gravity—the force that holds surfaces together. Each of us has an internal gravity, and the desire to escape it is the desire to escape the actuality of one's self. Insofar as community is real and valuable (and even a marriage is a community of two), the desire to escape, like the desire to fly, is both necessary and ruinous.

Furthermore, all human interactions are replicas of a few primal possibilities. The notion of freedom from any intense relationship is a dream. You are never free of your past. I have willy-nilly incorporated

———

E into myself, for example, and every so often she breaks out, in the form of a dismal sweat, all over me. Same with Montgomery Street.

When you start digging down into the roots of yourself, you find that you are not simply a self at all, but a maze of old relationships. With parents, neighbors, teachers, friends (meaning also enemies). That tangled and gnarled and overgrown past is your gravity, your form, which shapes everything in the present. What you see, what you do. All current struggles are endess variations on the primal, internal struggles from which we derive. Ourselves, that is.

So, in a sense, Z is my father.

But because the tangle is intricate, perhaps infinitely intricate, we can have at least the illusion of freedom, some room to maneuver.

I do not have to repeat with Z those old agonies.

This is all true and therefore banal when looked at directly.

Art is metaphor, and therefore interesting, not because of the truth the metaphor implies (always, in the end, a banality) but because of the infinite charm of the allusions themselves.

106

I can make a film about Montgomery Street and fill it with the stuff of my current experience; or I can make a film about that current experience and fill it with the stuff of Montgomery Street. It doesn't matter which way you work, so long as both ends are roughly equivalent to each other. And this equivalency, in any single life, is no trick, no mere Hollywood flashback servicing plot and sentiment. It's the feel, the sense, the texture of life itself.

Film records only surface, style. It can't "see" gravity. But if the style is precise and true, the mind will perceive the underlying form.

Freedom exists in life only to the extent that editing can change the implied form of bits of film. We are all limited to certain prerecorded actions—learned responses, the psychologist would say—but we can perform those bits of action in different sequences, and thus make them mean different, even brand-new and previously impossible things—the way Lumière "magically" made a mess of rubble assemble itself into a wall by merely reversing the original wall-crumbling shot. But no editor can create celluloid that wasn't there to begin with. Thus our freedom and our lack of it. Ultimately we are free only to the extent that we possess what must be called technical skill.

There has to be empathy between film-maker and viewer. Else you never leap the boundary between what the eye sees and the mind knows.

Which is why I must either make the movie I want to make, or make no movie at all.

Now all I have to be certain of is that *Montgomery Street* really is the film I want to do.

———

No, more than that, worse than that. It's like Stevie's desire to go to Chinatown. He opts for the action, the *doing;* but it's mostly Lester's company that he craves.

Look at how lonely I've made him, how alone. The fear of

107

touching and being touched, the desire. Dare he touch the mongoloid's arm?

Z is also playing out those old struggles.

Part of me wants to submit, film his damn book. Part of him wants me to buck him, insist on filming my film, be his—cohort.

How far are we going to go?

Never thwart your father too much. He may kill you.

Or worse, you may have to kill him.

———

Max will have spent a night like this. "Didn't sleep good," he'll tell his wife.

———

"The Style that Strikes the Eye is the True Style, But A Fool's Eye is Not to be a Criterion."

———

Self in time. Self aware of self in time, and so aware of rot, corruption, death. Self aware of limitations of self. (Can't fly.) Self aware of how much not-self self is: parents, friends, neighbors, culture, taboos, teachers, artifacts, books, movies, all prisms through which self considers self, all molds against which self forms self. Also self's memory of previous self. Self's hatred of extinction. Self's desire to expand, grow, become infinite, swallow the world. Self coming to fear self's desires. Self seeking to limit self. Conflict. In sex, love, art, death, madness, being lost, self becomes not-self. So those are the weapons of self against self.

———

Someone, probably Max, takes a piece of paper, draws a line down the middle, begins to list the pros and cons of some issue. Marriage/Divorce. Kennedy/Nixon. (We can't have both, but we did.) Life/Death.

———

Kids burning cats. A rock fight. Trying to hang a kid; he came home with a rope burn round his neck.

Samson and Delilah. Hair cut off. Man unmanned by lady barber. Victor Mature. What a name! Juvenile loser in a mirror.

The way you have to settle for less than the perfect, the recognition of one's own mortality.

Dealing with Z is like reading Blake. His candor is all subtlety. But anyway we've struck a deal. I go ahead with the project. He puts up a hundred thousand in seed money right away. I keep the production budget under two million, and I get the final cut. J's in with star billing. He gets casting veto on the main players. We sign a two-film contract, and verbally agree that selection of the second project will be by mutual consent. We also agree that *Montgomery Street* will get a PG rating even if cuts are necessary. (I'll have to be careful with the Nellie scene.) I choose the cinematographer; I control the sound track. I get 5 percent of the gross beyond production costs, with a delayed-payments clause written in. They like it, I get rich. I feel I'm floating a couple of inches above my chair, and it's not all elation. He wanted interiors to be filmed in England but I refused. The hell with his investments here! I'd sooner shoot in a warehouse on Fulton Street.

So it's done. We're committed. We're going out on the town tonight to celebrate. Now all I have to do is wait for the queasiness to go away.

Mort didn't sound surprised. He's been in cahoots with Z all along, of course. Doing what's best for me. I can practically hear them assuring each other that, really, artists are just like children, they need limits, someone watching them, some guidance as they go along.

I'm learning. Things I've known about all along. They just

don't seem to count until they've happened to you.

———

J: "It's going to be marvelous to work with you!"
Almost told her we could start right away.

———

How to use her? Wife or mistress? Did they actually have
mistresses, those gray men of Montgomery Street, hidden like
Benny's drunkenness, secret lives I knew nothing about?

Whatever her relation to Max, she'll have to be the woman
Stevie adores, a substitute for the rabbi's wife. I lose the religious
stuff that way, but I can bring it back by doing more with Korski.
Also Max. Introduce a rabbi. Maybe it's just as well. Good stuff is
never the result of mere license; it comes about in tension, the
struggle between countervailing forces. So J's the woman Stevie's
stuck on. That puts her in the grocery store as well as the delivery
scene. Maybe she can also be the customer who comes into the
candy store. She can haunt Stevie's morning, Max's night. She's
the connection between them. Fine. It's beginning to fall together now.

But be careful not to surrender to her world. Incorporate it,
embody it in mine, steal it if you have to, but don't allow her to
distort the story, sentimentalize Montgomery Street.

I can put her on the screen a lot, give her some good lines, but
she must remain the object of Stevie's/Max's perceptions. I don't
dare use her point of view.

———

You can often tell what's going on in a marriage by finding out
who washes the dishes.

———

She thinks women should have their consciousness raised the way
her mother probably thought women should have their hair
streaked. It's a matter of current fashion, being in vogue, arbitrary good taste.

———

110

She's no hot-eyed feminist, but you have to be careful with her: she's prickly.

—————

We are many selves, and our sense of singularity from moment to moment is a benevolent illusion—akin to the illusion of movie movement. What passes through the projector is nothing but a sequence of stills.

—————

Let her be his wife. Try it anyway and see what happens when you put her in. How would he feel about her? Why would she have married him? Because he is, after all, or was, virile. His baldness is a sign of it. Attraction of energies. She has drained him? Why has he failed in life? Or has he? Maybe in his own terms he is a success. Has gone *through* his youthful ambitions and opted for a return to Montgomery Street. Politics. Has come to Montgomery Street because that's where the people are. "The People." Couldn't abide the middle-class parlor pinks he had gone to school with; thinks of bohemians as parasites; the kind of radicalism, old Old Left, that in fact is deeply conservative. No, this is all out of focus.

Work backward from what can be seen.

—————

She's much younger than he is, youthful, vibrant, sexual. Artsy. Fifties Greenwich Village type uprooted, transplanted to banal Brooklyn. Reichian. Jungian. But she doesn't really read. She wants to stir up Montgomery Street, bring it back to what she thinks is life. Scene with Bertie Grossman: tries to convince her that a perfect orgasm would make her goiter go away. Has lovers. The street is scandalized by her. How would Max feel? I can't seem to get a fix on them; they're too made up.

—————

Women controlling, surrounding men. The female as the circle of civility in which men must learn to live. Being in the center of them, caught, trapped, stuck. Their centerpiece.

111

J to N.Y. on Thursday. Doing a teleplay for PBS, one of those "serious" and "timely" pieces about lesbianism. Told her we might as well fly home together.

Have the wife planning to go off somewhere, maybe to the Catskills, for the Labor Day weekend. "I've just got to get away." Max for some reason can't or won't come along. Gives him something else to brood about.

My father, yawning, on a Sunday evening: "I'm going to bed. Tomorrow is a labor day." The solace of working.

Keys. Too many keys. Max carries a ring full of keys, is always fumbling to find the right one. The only key Stevie has is the one that opens his own front door. A bit of pink ribbon tied to it. How as you get older you accumulate keys. Max finds an old key stashed away in a drawer and can't recall what lock it fits.

Have been reading through the researcher's report, immersing myself in that day. It's an exercise in serendipity, the pleasure of spotting random allusions and secret connections you never thought could be there, an old dead moment coming bit by bit to formal life. How much we forget; how little we notice, as we live it, the texture of a day.

Headlines from the *New York Times*, 9/2/60:

CONGRESS CLOSES;
UNABLE TO AGREE
ON SUGAR POLICY

A sweet rhyme! And this:

KHRUSHCHEV GOING
TO UN ASSEMBLY
WITH BLOC HEADS

Better recheck that one. Felicity (tell Mort to send her some roses) may have gotten it snarled in transmission.

It was the summer Elizabeth Taylor and hubby sailed off to Italy to begin filming *Cleopatra*. The summer of the Congo, the elections, the payola scandal—remember how they drove poor Alan Freed to death, murdered rock 'n' roll? That day the Pennsy railroad went on strike, promising monumental traffic jams for the holiday weekend coming up. The sun rose at 6:23 A.M., set at 7:28 P.M., just as Stevie was running from the cops. The weather was fair and warm, not too hot—the storm will have to be my own invention. A bright three-quarter moon shone on a clear evening.

Psycho had just opened, Tony Perkins with a fly on his hand, Janet Leigh in a trunk. Max, going to see it, would fear for himself.

Other films (have Stevie scan the newspaper ads): *The Lost World. End of Innocence. Bells Are Ringing. The Mating Game. Aren't We Wonderful?* Eddie Fisher: "Oh my papa, to me you were so wonderful; oh my papa, to me you were so grand." *Song Without End. Strangers When We Meet. Pay or Die. I'm All Right, Jack. The Savage Eye. The Smallest Show on Earth.*

B. Crowther, the old fud, reviewing *The Time Machine*, cannibal workers feeding upon flowery poets, a bizarre Hollywood resurrection. Rod Taylor and Yvette Mimieux. Serendipity.

The Dow Jones average closed Friday at 625.22, down 88 cents. Would anyone on Montgomery Street be interested?

Plays: *The Best Man, Five Finger Exercise, Toys in the Attic, The Sound of Music, The Miracle Worker, My Fair Lady, Take Me Along.* Music is a miracle worker. Please, fair lady, take me along.

In Yonkers, on Thursday, one Stanley Clifford Weyman was shot to death by a holdup man, who escaped. Weyman was working as a desk clerk in a hotel, though earlier in his life he had practiced as both a doctor and an attorney, a military officer and

113

a diplomat, the last of the great impostors.

The following Monday would bring a partial eclipse of the moon. Have someone talking about going up on the roof to watch it.

Shakespeare in the park: *The Taming of the Shrew.*

Baseball: Yanks played Orioles in Baltimore (lost 1-0)—a close pennant race, a big game.

How newsprint turns your fingers black.

From the now defunct *Mirror:*

300 SLAIN BY

CONGO ARMY

———

WINS $333

ON LUCKY 3

—11 OTHERS

COP PRIZES

Everything comes in threes. Willy bets on number three in the third. Morning, noon and night. Stevie, Max, and—what's her name?

"Let's Explore Your Mind." Cartoon of a melancholy boy, a woman in the background saying: "There's nothing as important as LOVE to a youngster."

Three carloads of police chased a monkey named George, who had escaped from a pet shop in Brooklyn. Before the cops cornered the beast he bit a boy playing stickball. Use it? Parody *King Kong?*

How to spot Echo I. A big silver ball of reflective foil floating up there.

Miss Rheingold. Make mine Ballantine.

The News:

K COMING HERE

THIS MONTH

Picture of a pretty girl, legs up on a suitcase, presumably waiting for a nonexistent train in empty Penn Station. The editorial: *Commies in the Congo.* Beloved Newstyle. Lumumba. Tshombe. Katanga. Like drumbeats. Wirephoto of blond Belgian waif terrorized at an airport. Waiting to escape from darkness, the same darkness that seemed to be seeping south from Bed-Stuy toward Montgomery Street. Paranoia. The UN in jungle. Negations. Guerrillas and gorillas. The heart of darkness staining black the pages of American newspapers, American minds. It's a hard rain's gonna fall. Huntley-Brinkley reports. Hunt for peace at the brink. UN in hunt in jungle. Un-American activities. I like Ike. Coons and coonskins. Davy Crockett. Killed him a bear when he was only three.

CITY'S THOUSANDS GET LOST

FOR THAT LAST WEEKEND

The Olympics. Late movie on Channel 7: *Out of the Clouds.* Those Million Dollar Movies on Channel 9. *Maverick. Have Gun, Will Travel.* Maybe I should marry Felicity if J won't have me. Playing off Broadway: *The Threepenny Opera.* Also *The Fantasticks, The Connection, Krapp's Last Tape.* Spike heels. Sack dresses. Ivy League pants—a belt in the back that holds up nothing. More movies: *Sons and Lovers, Beat the Devil, 400 Blows, M.* Hula Hoops. Yo-Yos. "The return of the tailfin?" Elvis becomes a GI, has his hair cut off. "Love Me Tender." "Don't Be Cruel." My cup runneth over.

———

How come she neglected the *N.Y. Post?*

———

Someone on the street is having a baby. In the synagogue they're preparing for a *bar mitzvah.* Across Empire Boulevard was the funeral parlor, marqueed like a movie theater, with dark-suited dark-eyed men directing the mourners' cars to line up behind the hearse. How we assumed they were *mafiosi.* Bringing a baby

115

home from the hospital. The neighbors oohing and ahing. Womb to tomb. "Isn't that the cutest thing you ever saw?" "What if tomorrow bring/sorrow or anything/other than joy?" How will the kid turn out? Is there a future? The cold war. Laos, Cuba, Berlin. Rockefeller wanting everyone to have an air raid shelter of his very own. Sirens going off at noon just to scare us all silly. Civil defense signs, yellow and black for dread and doom, arrows pointing you to the cellar. How airplanes terrified you at night. Stevie in bed hears a jet in the distance, terror comes. Any moment now we might all be annihilated. Folk singers' joke songs about it. The what-the-heck romanticism of the decade to come. Then the seventies, full circle. Quemoy-Matsu. Nixon and Kennedy are going to debate. Powers. U-2. Those Red Menace bubble gum cards we used to collect: Ivan in the salt mines. The ignorance of the place. Stevie is just beginning to be aware of politics, has an argument with someone, maybe Lester, about what? Something nonsensical. Lester proves to Stevie that Russia really hasn't sent any space satellites up. Or that it doesn't have any H-bombs. "If they had 'em, don't you think they'd use 'em, dope?" The superstitions of the place. How when Mrs. Kellerman ran for president of the PTA my mother said she must be a Communist. A picture of FDR on somebody's wall. Nostalgia for the bad old times. Eleanor Roosevelt is coming to give a talk at the school. "My Day." Veneration of idols, the avoidance of taboos. The tribal aspects of Montgomery Street. Kissing a prayer book, a *tallis*. Stevie's *tfillin*. *Yahrzeit*. Drinking water from a glass that once held a candle for the dead. Film as anthropology. How it must seem to us now as alien, as human, as Samoa.

Max Stein. Born 1919 in Brownsville. The clamor and bustle of push-carts now gone. Coming of age during the Depression, City College, left-wing politics. His father an old-line romantic anarchist, a fireman by trade. "I remember how he used to come home with the stink of smoke on him, coughing and spitting black smoke into the sink." Communism—he joined the party the way people nowadays take up TM, not really political, wants to be some kind of artist, maybe a sculptor. Then the war, the army somehow changing everything. Breakdown? Wounded? Comes home, gets a job, meets his wife—but remember, she's a lot younger than he is—the conventions of love and marriage which mock his past and settle his future. Those soap carvings. But why would he move to Montgomery Street? He was on the verge of some kind of success—show biz? radio? TV?—then comes the McCarthy period, black lists, the secrets of the past dredged up. Montgomery Street is his sanctuary.

Dry, no juice in it, parched as England. It will be good to get home.

When you worry about what you are, about the connection of your current life to your remembered past (of which some unknown portion is just an illusion), you end up going in circles; you get trapped trying to remain what you've been, or think you've been, in the flux of the future. The collision of old forms of existence with the new demands of the present moment. The sense of being out of time, untimely, a stranger to the day. Something has to happen to help you break through. In Max's case—a mistress? the gun? someone's death?

Home. Home sweet home. I walked through the door, my mind filled with the gorgeousness of the flight, a vision of the sun setting like a dim candle where the horizon curved away into a blue mist of sky and sea, and found my apartment had been burglarized. Vandalized might be more accurate, though my stereo rig is missing, and a shelf of art books, and no doubt a lot of other things. Or maybe while I was gone the place was simply inhabited by a couple of sticky-fingered slobs. Miserably depressing. I felt like just walking away from the mess and starting all over again somewhere else. Serves me right, I suppose. You can't

117

go away and leave a place standing empty for more than two months, not in this town. But why slash the sofa? Why break dishes? Why step out cigarettes on the rug? Why, having relieved yourself, leave the goddam toilet unflushed? The sick familiar feeling of having your home contaminated, made strange—dogs must feel that way sniffing another dog's piss on their favorite fire plug. The loss of the sanctity of possession, the dread that none of this is mine any more. Like being cuckolded. The feeling we had when the Pigtowners came around "our" schoolyard. Is nothing sacred any more, is nothing safe? The bastards! The filthy gloating bastards!

I'm sick about it. I'm sitting here thinking I'd like to go out and find them, hunt them down, kill them—but though the rage is real, the thought is inauthentic, a pose, a result of seeing too many revenge movies.

Do we find ourselves in films, or do films in some way actually create the selves we are?

The bastards!

———

Some day this has been. Burglars leave an opening in your life and all sorts of other intruders come pouring through. First a couple of clownish cops, looking the place over with professional indifference, scribbling in their notebooks, patiently explaining what I already know, that there's little chance of justice being done. Then the insurance man, making sure the criminal isn't me. Then a couple of jokers from Allied Maintenance, with their roaring industrial vacuum cleaner and their awful disinfectants. And while they were still here the upholsterer showed up to haul away the couch. Then the deliveryman bringing the new stereo rig—without which I just can't feel at home. Finally my neighbor the tax attorney popped in to tell what a bonanza a burglary can be. "It's all deductible, you know." I knew. I had already talked to my mother. She told me.

So, among other things, they have stolen a day from my life.

It's colder in New York than it was in London, an early fall creeping up on us. They're predicting a harsh winter. In Westchester County, according to the *Times*, the chipmunks have grown wondrously fat and fluffy. I went to the closet to haul out my suede jacket and my suede jacket was gone. And through it all I keep remembering: I've got a movie to do.

Called E. We chatted about the burglary. She hoped that I had had a good time in France. I told her I wanted to see the kids next weekend, maybe take them to the zoo. "How unimaginative," she said. I'm proud of myself. I didn't let it become a squabble.

Slowly, my life is returning to order, the place is re-acquiring my own scent. I have gone so far as to unpack my suitcase and stow it away in the closet. Something pathetic about it, empty and tossed in a corner. It seemed almost to complain; it wants to go back to Sète, which in memory seems already to be trimmed and burnished and adorned with bright colors. Maybe I should buy a summer house there, start a trend. Some joke. The crazy thing is that I'm still not used to the fact that I can afford to do it, that I have money to burn. The neighbors should see me now.

I have also packed away in a carton the clutter of *Centerpiece*, clearing my desk for the new clutter of *Montgomery Street*. It's nice to have a typewriter handy again, but also dangerous. My desire is to start pounding out a script, or at least an outline, commit myself, get something on paper for Z. But I'm still not sure who Max is, or how he will spend the day.

Dinner party at Mort's last night. The usual crowd of lawyers and agents. His wife looks like hell. There are troubles there I know nothing about. Never will, either.

Everyone, of course, having swallowed qualms, was working for Carter. But I had the feeling they weren't too happy about it.

They can't quite get over their superstitions, the agnostic's dread of the believer's power and magic. It's the same fear I felt as a kid whenever I passed a church. Careful: there's strong, alien, *goyische* enchantment there. Or that time I found a New Testament in the schoolyard and hid it among my comic books, afraid that should I dare to open it, read a few verses, I'd be damning my soul. And then that summer with E, our first time in Europe, visiting every church on the Continent, it seemed, and the shimmer of guilt which eventually waned and vanished. Hard to believe how much you can change, how very far I really am from Montgomery Street.

———

Max quite literally sees a different Montgomery Street than Stevie does. What remains blurred, mere background in the Stevie sections, comes sharply into focus in Max's scenes, and vice versa. They are antithetical and yet singular, reflections of each other, matter and antimatter, flip sides of the same metaphysical coin. Stevie's world is yellow, red, green; Max's is brown, gray, black. The black of the gun he finds. The black and white of newsprint versus the rainbow colors of comic books. Stevie loves sweets, Max sours and bitters—he eats salami, pickle, beer. Stevie, walking, sees, attaches himself to, sky, sun, clouds, rooftops. Max, slowly bending round with age and worry, fixes his eyes on pavement, gutters, the all-too-solid ground. Stevie is fascinated by mirrors; the uncertain vanity of adolescence, is always contemplating his reflection in a store window. Max dislikes mirrors—the way he dislikes being mistaken for someone else—fears and hates the loss of singularity, the way they seem to replicate him. Maybe at some point in the day he breaks one.

None of which gives me much in the way of action, events, scenes to shoot. He's not going to be easy.

———

His wife. Call her Elinor, Ellie, El. Bohemian, at least by Brooklyn standards. The sort of woman who would parade along

Montgomery Street in shorts and a halter, mimicking the teen-agers, just to make the neighbors gawp. How will J look in a ponytail? A few streaks of premature gray in her hair—she hasn't had an easy life. Thirtyish, eighteen when she married Max. He's almost a decade older than she is. She is also ambitious in her way. But what does she *do?*

Her problem is that she doesn't do anything. She has fallen into sloth. Blames it on the street, on Max. "If only—" Somehow her parents left her with a sense of specialness, of being a princess fallen among peasants. The way she puts on airs. A whiff of decadence, of domestic tragedy far in the background.

Her father was one of those hot-eyed Zionists who mingled in his mental baggage the pain of exile, Spinoza, communal ideals, free love. In temperament she takes after him. He killed himself, messily, when she was twelve. She was, when Max met her, a thin pathetic waif, moody, shadowed. He found this romantic. But she has fed on him, grown healthy and strong.

Her mother was a weak woman, completely overshadowed by her father; she is determined not to be like her. Max's case is, to some extent, the opposite.

The way we struggle against our own inevitable natures.

She spends a lot of the day in bed. She sunbathes on the roof. Music? She was going to be a singer, has worked in cheap nightclubs. Is "between jobs."

Can J sing?

She soothes herself with psychosexual theories of all kinds, believes that all troubles, mental and physical, originate in bed. She likes four-letter words for their shock value. That scene in the candy store—trying to convince Bertie Grossman to make Willy perform in bed. She is, or maybe once was, entangled in a messy affair with a pseudo artist from Greenwich Village. She has been known not to come home for days at a time. The neighbors think she's a "tramp." Maybe that night she goes to a Village party

121

from which Max has to extricate her, arriving just ahead of the cops. He is horrified by her excesses. She sticks out. Korski sends Stevie up with some stale rolls or yesterday's milk, and she marches right down and loudly demands a refund. She's a passionate, determined, crusading atheist; she goes to the synagogue to argue theology and flirt with the young, indulgent rabbi. Someone talks about how she walked down the street on Yom Kippur eating a jelly apple, bright and red as a beacon. All of which torments Max. His impulse is to blend with the scenery, hide himself. A chameleon: his language, for example, tends to take on the tone and accents of the person he's talking to.

Her sweet tooth. A perennial box of chocolates at her bedside. All over the house, those crinkly brown paper cups. Loves big syrupy ice cream concoctions. Energy, a metabolism gone wild— nothing she eats will ever make her fat.

She is constantly succumbing to frills and fancies and feminine trifles. She's a rearranger, never satisfied. "I've been thinking of redoing the sofa." "I'm so tired of those old drapes." We see her in a kind of frenzy changing pictures from wall to wall— she likes impressionism, pseudo pointillistic junk. Max, entering the living room, stubs his toe on an unexpected chair. She comes into the store, demands he give her some new piece that has caught her eye.

"Look, please, try to understand. This is my business. This is how I make my living."

"Okay, okay, never mind. I'll live without it."

"You're driving me crazy—you know that, don't you, Ellie? You're sending me to the nuthouse!"

The sense of old conflagrations still smoldering between them.

She tries to erect around herself a perfection of style that always eludes her. Thus she is always complaining, always unhappy about something or another. Poor guilty Max, always feeling he's to blame.

"Now what's the matter?"

"Nothing. Nothing at all."

"Don't say nothing. Tell me what's the matter!"

"Nothing's the matter. I'm just fine!"

Flaring up: "For crine out loud, what do you want from me!"

Too easy? Too much like me? Too much like every marriage I know? But Montgomery Street was, on the surface, all cliché.

He has to be a match for her. He has to be strong, funny, vigorous. A kibitzer. A kind of disillusioned wisdom that gives him an air of solidity, authority. The sort of man people turn to in moments of crisis. Despite his mute turmoil, he has struggled through to simple common sense. He has a strong stomach. When the old lady jumped off the roof, Max was the obvious choice to hose down the sidewalk. The "good" father Stevie never had.

She has recently taken an interest in the civil rights movement. Has been reading Mailer. Her upside-down racism, envying blacks their energy, their physicality, their rhythm. "I wanna be able to shake my ass, that's all. I just wanna shake my goddam ass." Maybe has a fantasy about going down to Mississippi, sitting in at Woolworth's.

Realistic Max: "For what you want, you don't have to go to Mississippi."

"And I've got two words for you, too, buster."

She can be mean, real mean.

For Max the world is a series of mysteries one is obligated to try to make sense of; for Ellie it's a lump of clay to be molded according to whim, remolded according to fashion. Her deepest desire is to imprint herself upon the world the way movie stars used to place their handprints in Hollywood sidewalks. "I want people to know I'm here!" Thus, what she can't understand, she immediately dislikes; what she finds burdensome (her marriage,

123

for example) she tries to destroy. But she is, like any of us, always shying away from her own worst nature.

Max believes their marriage is a war of opposing principles; in fact, much of the time, they are painfully the same.

Which is why she frightens him. And that's what holds them together.

Their marriage seems always on the verge of dissolution, but it isn't really. They are bound together like the poles of a magnet, they will go on with their squabbling forever. Because on Montgomery Street there can be no change, no sudden influx of cash or new friends or soaring expectations, to disrupt the pattern. Besides, he adores her. He is in thrall to her energy, her vitality, her earthiness. He hates it, too. Thus the tension in which he must live.

And her? Don't forget, times have changed. She can't imagine herself (as J so easily can) living beyond the circle of marriage, home, permanence, a reliable man. She can fantasize it, but she can't live it. Because she's afraid. She knows, had learned from her father, that you can cross the lines all right, but not with impunity. There's always danger, there's always the possibility of pain and madness and death, and so there is always fear. Nowadays it has become fashionable to confess the fear, to parade our anxiety, but then, there, on Montgomery Street, to be afraid was to be ashamed.

So they keep each other in check. Each of them believes they have been forced to live within the limits of the other, each of them dreams of the exotic life they could lead if only the other would disappear. In fancy, they are always on the verge of annihilating each other, but they are both terrified by their own imaginings—that line in Borges: the man awakening in the middle of the night to strangle the woman asleep beside him— and so each little murder is followed by a little resurrection. It's a Punch and Judy show—they keep knocking each other down so they can feel the comfort of watching each other get up again.

Love. They do, they love each other, that quiet, edgy, ruinous love, unromantic, unconfessed, the fruit of a long marriage. A love covered with the scar tissue of old wounds and unresolved grievances and simple, maddening incompatibilities. My love for E even now. The hurt she can still cause me.

Because there was for both of them, in the beginning, a moment of formidable, unrepeatable, immemorial bliss. Perhaps that Friday should be the anniversary of it.

She's sloppy, romantic, "natural." He's a city man through and through. He has no use for trees and flowers; he hates those weekend gambols through the Botanic Garden that Ellie adores. He has hay fever—sneezing, eyes watering, watching the pollen count. The beginning of September is the height of the season. "Thank God for the rain!" He is squeamish about the big flat black insects he's always finding in the bathtub. "Nature? I'll tell you what nature is, my dear. Nature is bugs and beasts and Buchenwald!" He loves the man-made and artificial—the power station on Nostrand Avenue, the grime of it, the red brick, the hum of all that trapped and focused and productive energy. "Keep it in check!" is his motto. Let it loose and chaos comes.

He is one of those vanished, pre-ecological types, in love with plastics and plumbing and the regularity of pavement. The miracles of medicine—glass eyes, prosthetic limbs, transplanted kidneys, open-heart surgery—these (have him tell someone; a scene in a hospital?) are emblems of all that's good. *Ben Casey* on TV. Those fierce eyes smoldering behind the hygienic mask.

He believes you have to impose pattern and order on the turbulence of life; it doesn't matter what pattern, what order—the point is to fashion the world in your own image. Thus his old flirtation with communism; what drew him was the arbitrary rigidity of it, the illusion of understanding and the promise of self-discipline. Thus the agony of his soap-carving, images spawned of his deepest turmoil, unknown, unconfessed. Thus his terror when he finds the gun. Watching the workers rip up the sidewalk; a shiver of symptomatic dread.

Thus also his connection to machines. He is at his happiest when he is plucking apart a malfunctioning electrical gimcrack, setting out upon his workbench the screws and bolts and wired innards, tracing through the maze of the circuit for the loose wire, the broken connection, the worn washer that caused the thing to jam. He has a passion for light and light bulbs, the miracle of that filament blazing in a vacuum.

Home, evening: "What are you sitting here in the dark for?"

"I like the dark."

He puts on a light. She blinks at him, all agony.

The mess of their apartment. He struggles haplessly against her slovenly ways.

He is up on the latest technology. Reads *Scientific American*, *Popular Mechanics*. Adores the newfangled notion of computers. Glories in space exploration, sputniks, Vanguards, all that exquisite junk wheeling in space, sterile, perfect, beyond the whims of weather, gravity, corruption.

"It says in the paper if you go out at nine-thirty and look west you can see Echo II."

But all of this must seem, in part, an affectation. He is a big sprawling sloppy sort of man always struggling to contain himself.

He scoffs at what he calls "the sentiments of family life" and believes he is bothered not at all by the sterility of their marriage; they are one of the few childless couples on the block. But this may be a key to his disconnection.

Anyway, some of the basic elements are there.

———

We see Stevie in fluid long shots, a moving camera, his spontaneity; we see Max caught in close-ups, a stationary camera, trapped by the frame, almost about to burst it. For Stevie the world is all vistas and horizons; with Max the sense of walls closing him in.

126

He may even at times seem to be almost aware of the camera's proximity, how he's caught and squeezed and trapped between the plane of some wall behind him and the plane of the screen in front of him. Remind them that in film the third dimension is an illusion. The screen as reflector, glass bead games, a million mirrors.

Z has taken out half a page in *Variety* to announce *Montgomery Street.* "Stephen Mandreg" and "Joyce Jerome" are both in the same size type. "An affectionate tribute to Brooklyn in the late 1950s." Affectionate tribute? Sure, why not? I loved the damn place despite everything, didn't I?

Took the girls to the park yesterday, and then to the Museum of Natural History. Managed to convince J to come along, and she turned out to be as ebullient and practiced as the old camp counselor she is. I think they liked her. The afternoon was all balloons and ice cream cones and the vague tension of unmentionable topics, every "Mommy" a little stab. Cindy, wide-eyed, at the bones of a brontosaurus: "Were there dinosaurs around when you were little, Daddy?" Yes, my precious, I'm old, I'm old. But they are thriving without me nevertheless.

Max's day. Wakes up out of a terrible night. They've had some kind of bitter argument—he's been cuckolded once too often? His loathing, his fear. Dresses, breakfast, some kind of scene between them. Out on the street. The workman ripping up the sidewalk, the jagged roar of the jackhammer. Finds the gun. Where? In his shop, contemplating it. Does Bono fit in here? A phone call. Going off to Brownsville to buy up some furniture. The slum Montgomery Street will become. Lunch. How does he spend the afternoon? How does it relate to the Stevie scenes? Still not clear.

One of those mornings when you sit and stare and listen down the corridors of memory and inspiration, and nothing comes, nothing at all, and everything starts seeming sour, banal, drab.

"Everything is possible in history; triumphant, indefinite progress equally with periodic regression. For life, individual and collective, personal or historic, is the one entity in the universe whose substance is compact of danger, of adventure. It is, in the strict sense of the word, drama."

ORTEGA

To the movies with J last night. The new Hitchcock. She adored it; I was depressed. We have reached the point where I can allow myself to be depressed with her. We're becoming great pals, all right, such good friends. She's no doubt wondering what I'm waiting for. I wonder myself. Curious, really, the pleasant tension you can conjure up between yourself and a woman when you don't allow sex to intrude. Obverse, I suppose, of the old tensions of adolescent dating: how far will I get, how far does she go? Or the exquisite tension of cooking a fine meal—we ate here, my special stew—and not stealing a taste from the pot, waiting for the wine to be poured, the table set. Strange conjunction: I keep thinking lately that I can get on the subway and be in Brooklyn in less than an hour. I have even dreamed about it—though in my dream I came up out of the station and found myself in an unfamiliar, alien neighborhood. Is this why I'm so reluctant to go, because it is changed beyond recognition? Or am I afraid it hasn't changed enough, and that seeing what's left of it will somehow abolish my memories, my imagination. If I'm going to shoot on location, maybe I'd better plan on finding locations I need in the Bronx. I feel sure that to film what remains of an actual Montgomery Street will catch nothing at all of the street I wish to create. Or am I simply, again, deferring a certain pleasure for the promise of a greater pleasure to come? The

128

reality principle. Thank you, doc. Anyway, unless Max comes clear, there'll be nothing to film at all. Quite a struggle he's giving me, old Maxie Stein.

The gun. The crisis. Somehow it's resolved. He's not going to shoot anyone after all. Goes to the police station to turn the thing in. Scene with a detective. They bring in some poor colored boy all beat up. When he leaves the police station he's drawn— why?—to the synagogue across the street. Friday-night services. Only the regulars turn out for it. How many of them were authentically religious: how many were using it as an excuse to get away from wife and home? Max in the synagogue. That intense feeling, all mingled old memory and current strangeness. Fingering a prayer book. You're supposed to kiss it. A scene with the rabbi? "Max, it's never too late fo find God." "It's not exactly God I'm looking for." The *shammus* in his white suit, the little beard, looking like Charlie Chan. A boy preparing for his *bar mitzvah*, the scrubbed devotion of the twelve-year-old which would turn into scruffy skepticism by the time he's fourteen. Old man wrapped in a *tallis*, swaying, murmuring the age-old chants. In the end Max walks away from it. Home again. Long scene with his wife, some kind of argument. Interrupted by a hysterical neighbor—her husband's having a heart attack. Max has to go with him to the hospital. Death. He comes home in the small hours of Saturday morning, then in bed with his wife. A kind of reconciliation; the mere animal warmth of their bodies together in bed, the ambiguous comfort of it, a final note of utmost simplicity. Another day. Nothing more.

Max, morning, Montgomery Street: what does he see? what does he know? That the buildings on the street have names as well as numbers, the irony of it, *Montgomery Castle* stamped in concrete above the doorway, pan up to the bleak windows tangled in fire escapes. Scene with the neighbor who will later on have the heart attack, a dismal old man, trembling hands, wet eyes, a lost and fugitive soul. "You look like you're guarding the street, Morris!" "You maybe got something better for me to do?"

In Max's POV: garbage cans spilling their contents, melon rinds, moldy bread, old magazines, a broken alarm clock; the iron fences, painted thick bubbly black over rust; a battered old shoe lying in the gutter; that neighbor with the new car; Jeremy picking his nose; maybe a glimpse of Lester. Then Nostrand Avenue, bustling and commercial: black smoke belching from the exhaust pipe of a bus; a pile of broken orange crates in front of the fruit store; the burned out, boarded-up drugstore; a *Hasidic* rabbi with a big round fur hat, carrying an incongruous attaché case; Bono's delivery bike in front of Waldbaum's; the grime that collects on the edgings of windows; bits of glass. His store: "Oddz & Endz." Next to it is a Chinese laundry, two skinny little kids loitering in the doorway, the steamy dimness within. He says good morning to them; as always, they shy away.

Max fumbling for a key, finds the right one, fumbles to get it in. A comic bit, every morning's insane ritual. The door sticks: he has to hammer it at a certain point, then pull upward and lean his weight "just so" in order to get it opened. Doors don't yield easily to Max. When the door opens a burglar alarm goes off. He has to rush into the store and find the switch to silence the damn thing. The blare of it troubles him, makes him feel he has broken in.

He lurches into the store, stumbling over a package he hasn't noticed. Shuts off the alarm, comes back, bangs his head on the doorknob when he stoops to pick the package up.

Rubs his head with one hand, holds the package in the other, hefting its considerable weight. Ends up with a small scratch marring that perfect bald dome of his.

The shop. The clutter of it like the clutter of memory, impossible to sort out, though Max knows by intuition and practice just where everything is. He's no bumbler, despite the slapstick. There's order in the apparent jumble. "I can't explain it, but believe me, I've got a system."

(Later a customer comes in: "I'm looking for stereopticon cards." "No problem; they're right over there.")

Dolly shot through the store. Linger on the surfaces and textures. Max's workbench. The array of beloved tools. He puts the package down and the telephone rings.

Stay tight on the package, which is next to the phone—make it one of those old-fashioned upright phones: "I remember those!" Max's hand plucking up the receiver. Tighter on the package; his hand toying carelessly with the heavy twine.

We hear Max arranging to go to Brownsville later that day to look over some "stuff."

His hand picks up a pencil and scribbles an address on the package. He rips off that piece of the wrapping. Exposes just enough so we can see it's a gun.

His voice changes. He quickly completes the conversation, hangs up.

Now slowly pull back as Max sits down at the workbench, stares at the package. A long, long breath. Looks up. Goes to the door and locks it. Returns to the bench. Cuts the cord with a penknife. Unwraps it with slow and exquisite precision as though it were about to explode.

High angle, looking down at Max, the top of his head, the gun. Make it a big dull-black automatic, like the guns Wilmer used in *The Maltese Falcon*.

Another angle: tight on Max's face. Runs his hand over his bald skull, wincing as he fingers the scratch.

Picks the gun up with two fingers, gingerly. Breathing heavily. Maybe the faint echo of his pounding heart on the sound track. For a moment, as he holds the gun in his right hand, he's pointing it at himself; then his left hand comes up and pushes the muzzle away.

Puts the gun down, turns it over, examines it some more.

Makes his hand into a gun, index finger extended, pointing more or less at the camera.

Max, softly, to himself, as he squeezes the imaginary trigger: Pow, pow, pow.

Cut to Stevie in the candy store reading that book.

———

Later that morning, exterior, Max's store. A black kid maybe eighteen years old, wearing one of those bop caps that were just beginning to be stylish then, raincoat, sneakers. Nervous. Skulking. Looks in the doorway, walks past the store, turns, walks back, indecisive, finally goes in.

Interior: Max with a handkerchief, sneezing, his hay fever acting up.

The kid. He's obviously not interested in antiques.

Max mops his brow. "Can I help you?"

"Could be, could be."

On the kid; he's staring at the antiques as though they were artifacts shipped down from another planet.

M: Well?

Kid (very jumpy): I'm just looking around, man.

M: Anything in particular?

Kid: Yeah, something very particular . . . You know how sometimes someone loses something, and then, you know, man, someone else finds something?

M (controlling himself): I'm not a fence, if that's what you mean.

Tight on the kid, thinking things over, his face screwed up with the effort of concentration.

Kid: I mean, like, you know, someone maybe has to put something down for a minute, and someone else picks it up.

M: I don't know what you're talking about.

Kid gives Max probing look.

Kid: You don't derive my meaning?

Max: I'm sorry, but I'm very busy . . .

A beat.

Kid (reaching a decision): Must be talking to the wrong man.

Gives Max one final probing look and leaves.

On Max as he watches him go. A breath, a smile—then a sneeze.

Later the kid is in the police station; Max pretends not to recognize him, doesn't mention him to the cops.

Scene: a woman enters the store, red hair done up in a beehive, lots of make-up, archetype of the Brooklyn Jewish matron. She is carrying a battered old chalice, baroquely ornate, a design of fruits and branching foliage and birds and angels.

Woman: Just have a look at this, Max. My son takes a trip to Europe, the big shot, and look what he brings me home. You think maybe it's worth something?

Max examines it, taps it with a fingernail: It's not silver, if that's what you mean.

Woman: So what then?

Max: Some kind of alloy. Mostly tin. Here, look, it's molded. You can see on the bottom the line where the two halves come together.

W: So what am I going to do with it?

Max shrugs.

W: I was thinking maybe it would make a nice lamp. You could maybe gild it and wire it for me.

M: If that's what you want.

W: So what's it going to cost?

Etc. Keep it brief.

When she's gone he puts the thing down on his workbench, looks at it, plunks it again with his fingernail, shakes his head in dismay at the whole wide world of bad taste.

There's not enough tension in it. Somehow I haven't made the

gun register. Have to show the pressures building on Max. Max
with the landlord, needs money; Max with some big-shot Manhattan antique dealer, aware of limits of his own dreary world;
Max with his wife; Max becoming afraid he will use the gun, kill
somebody.

———

Brownsville where Max grew up, now a slum. A littered schoolyard with brown and black children at play. A small mountain of
garbage. Familiar advertisements oddly transfigured by Spanish
lettering. A *bodega*. An old torn couch on the sidewalk. The
elevated train to New Lots Avenue rumbling by overhead; the
flickering shadows beneath. Boarded-up stores. A wino asleep in
a doorway. An abandoned car, bashed, stripped of its tires. Black
men lounging on a stoop, watching Max go by: their amused,
menacing, lizard eyes. A cop car, a pair of anxious cops. The
cliché of slum children playing in the torrent of an open fire
hydrant. An old white-haired Jewish lady staring out from
behind a barred window. A dark-red stain on the sidewalk—the
possibility of blood. A Puerto Rican teen-ager wearing a Dracula
cape. A black transvestite in a blond wig, bright-red rouged
cheeks. A teen-ager, running ferociously for no apparent reason,
almost knocks Max down. Don't say anything; just keep walking;
look straight ahead. Vitality, despair. A demented middle-aged
black man, talking to himself, carrying on a bitter argument with
his internalized, omnipresent wife. Graffiti on walls like territori-
al droppings: "Lords," "Skulls." Loud Latin music from a radio
in a window up above. A little brown bird pecking at a crusted
bone.

Max enters a building. A filthy hallway, the usual flights of
stairs, three apartments to a landing; dark areas where light bulbs
have burned out. Peeling walls. The remains of a once fancy
chandelier. The smell of piss tingling in Max's nose.

As he goes up, a black woman in a shocking-pink kimono
opens a door and looks at him, teasing, smirking, playing with

134

her collar. The blare of her hot dark nakedness coming through. Max goes past her, turns to look at her, throws her a kiss. Her sullen congested aggressive invitation softens into a friendly smile.

Max continues on up.

He—

———

Give him an affair, a fling, a moment of heat with that black woman? Let him live Stevie's fantasies? The absorbed power of that gun? Maybe have that person he's going to buy the furniture from be a woman, a suburban housewife, Madame Bovary type. Selling off her parents' belongings gives her a sense of freedom— "They're dead now, now I can live!"— so she seduces the junkman.

But sex is Stevie's preoccupation. Max's mind that morning in on the gun, on his marriage, on time and aging, violence and death.

Let it go.

———

A busy dapper little man in a silk business suit, fresh haircut, cufflinks, a big expensive wristwatch, probably a stockbroker or insurance salesman, a success—one of those ignoramuses who make of a handshake a test of virility. Just-barbered look. Max, feeling shabby, scruffy, gets a whiff of aftershave.

Familiar story, familiar sort of apartment. After thirty-five years—"You know how it is, they had to stay in the old neighborhood"—his father died, his mother, in mute despair and loneliness, acquired the symptoms of senility, so they packed her off to a nursing home. Now it's time to "close up" the place, sell off the property. It's just a nasty bit of business for him and he's in a hurry to close the deal. Keeps looking at his watch. "Listen, I have to be back uptown at twelve-thirty." No qualms, no attachment to his past.

"Look, I know the ropes, I went through this *mishagas* with my wife's parents. I know you're going to rob me. So you're going to rob me. Let's get it over with."

Vague parody of the ferocity and energy of James Cagney in *One, Two, Three.*

As they go through the house they have the air of burglars who can't find anything worth stealing.

"That television is practically new. Bought it for them just last year."

Max, rudely: I don't buy televisions.

What I want is a sense of desolation; the shabby sofa, the worn carpets, the sagging bed, the faded dishes; the way abandoned objᶜcts tend to become unreal, as though they existed solely through the lives of their owners. The way the fellow's surrendering of his past destroys its value. Contrast to Max's antiques, which give off, because of his attachment to them, a sense of expectancy, of a life to come.

In the living room there is a cabinet filled with dolls. These interest Max.

"Who collected the dolls?"

"My mother. Some of them must be pretty old, worth a few bucks."

Max's POV, panning the dolls, a kind of counterpart to his soap carvings.

He picks one up, turns it over, inspects its behind beneath a flouncy faded skirt.

Max: She had good taste, your mother.

For a moment the man lets go his sharp expression, a softness shows through, quickly repressed.

"I figured they'd be worth something."

Max is disgusted.

The man looks at his watch.

"So make me your best offer and let's be done with it."

"Well, I'll tell you. The dolls I can use. Maybe some of the kitchen stuff, the silver. As for the rest, I'd have to pay someone to cart it off, and maybe if I'm lucky I break even."

"Okay, sure, but what numbers are we talking?"

"Three hundred dollars for the lot."

"You're kidding."

"Listen, my friend, you call up the Salvation Army, you know what they tell you. You wait two months for an appointment and then they do you a big favor and take the stuff away."

And so on. It's all right. Needs maybe one more element. Have the guy recognize Max? They grew up together?

"Say, didn't you go to Boys' High?"

Better: "Say, I know you. You grew up around here, didn't you?"

"Right around the corner."

"Yeah, I remember you. Sure. You used to hang around with Sollie Levine, the one they sent to jail. Said he was a Commie."

"I knew Sollie."

"No kidding. You remember Mickey Grossman? He used to run with your pack."

"Sure, I knew Mickey."

"Mickey married my sister."

"Is that right? Well, how is he?"

"Oh, Jesus, he's been dead for ten years now. Jumped in front of a train."

A moment of communion over lost time. Broken when the fellow looks at his watch. How does he manage it, that shaking off of the past? For Max it is all vivid and relentless and terrible.

———

Party last night. J at my side like an ace up my sleeve. I wonder if it seems to her that I am showing her off, parading her, using her as an emblem of my energy and luck. She is the very essence of how far I've come from drab Montgomery Street. Which is also, I suppose, the crux of my problem. People kept asking me about my new project, and I mouthed some generalities, putting on my boldest, cockiest face—but behind it I started feeling ever more queasy and heartsick and unconvinced. "A movie about Brooklyn? Isn't that interesting!" Meaning, of course, that it isn't. Bad vibes. The way you could see them thinking about it, adding up the loss. Are they right?

I'm beginning to believe that it was only the distance of Sète that made it seem exotic. Now that I'm back in New York, where every other nose is a Brooklyn nose, and where you hear on every side the low-comedy accents of my hackneyed youth, my thoughts seem trivial and dull. A movie about Brooklyn? A movie about nothing more than a nice Jewish boy learning sex and love and money and the limits of dreams, and a nice Jewish man torn by morbidity and the pain of self-consciousness and a gun that will never go off—who cares? Where's the spectacle, the glamor, the heroics, the thrill, the dream that pulls them in? Where, for that matter, is the truth of it? Is it going to turn out to be the kind of movie I myself would want to see? Aren't I relying too much on the glitter of technique and style and random cleverness? Isn't it hollow at the heart of it? Or worse, boring?

Where's the hook?

How much can I count on sight gags and the drollness of recognition?

I'm just not sure about this thing.

The trouble seems to be that I could remember the tone and sense, the details of Stevies's life, but I'm having to concoct Max out of the bits and shards of secondary imagination. I still can't quite see what's there. His wife, the gun, his naked baldness, his figurines, his antiques. Lots of ideas but no life blood. That's why he keeps going in and out of focus, as though he were merely a creature of my moods. I'm groping. One moment he is quivering with indignant vitality (and then he seems a kind of angry little squirrel of a man chattering at a pigeon, protecting a fat nut), the next he seems stifled and glum, smoldering, inarticulate, hapless, like my father. I can't really feel him, or maybe don't want to.

The notion that making Max is, in a sense, to fix my own future. That gun. How *does* he feel about it? If he's been in the war, it can't seem as alien, as threatening, as it does to me.

———

I keep thinking of that black woman in the pink kimono, the half-open door, the smoky light, the muss of an unmade bed, her aggressive invitation, the antithesis, I suppose, of the rabbi's wife. Give Max a plunge into that fabulous darkness?

———

He's impotent. Max is impotent. There it is: not cuckoldry, but impotence. The impotence of Montgomery Street. That sense of shriveling, smallness, softness. Connects in his mind to death and suicide. The gun, the steely hardness he lacks. Play with the obviousness of the symbols. It's what has fouled his marriage. It haunts his day. The pre-potence of Stevie and the post-potence of Max, and the suggestion of a potency above and beyond, controlling things. Ellie wouldn't want to be stuck with an impotent husband—her philosophy forbids it! But don't be clinical. That sense of powerlessness, of a world too vast and dark and threatening. Look how it all falls together—his gloom, his fear of nature, the torment of the gun, that sense of a hard protective shell around a core of shameful softness. His guilt. His unconvincing swagger. Impotence as a state of mind. The previous night they've had a bad scene about it. He's been through hell. "What can I tell you, I'm not a young man any more." Attaches to the problem of time, aging. He feels old, used up. The way the street has grown old, used up. "I'm sorry, I just don't have it any more."

They don't have to discuss it; it remains hidden in the day, so obvious it need never be mentioned. The unspoken core which all the detail points to.

———

Max in his shop; some friend of his, one of the neighboring merchants, comes in to show off a new pinup poster.

"Wouldya look at the pair of ka-nockers on her!"

139

Max struggling to keep up the artifice of sexual banter.

The counterpoint of virility, in Max's day. Thick-armed garbage-men pouring trash into the huge maw of a truck. Bono and his bike. The confident hardness of the fellow in Brownsville.

Isn't it too easy, and too pathetic? What happens to the bold, strong Max?

I've been sitting here thinking: If impotence, then what?—and somehow what ought to follow doesn't come. It's no good. I've lost the thread of it. It's as though the thought dissolved the image I had of Max, and so of the picture.

Look at it. Impotence as a kind of hydraulic malfunction is the stuff of soap opera. The fear of it, being universal, is more interesting, but banal. The point has to lie not in impotence but in the metaphors it suggests.

American film is a series of images of potency. The cowboy, the gangster, the detective, the dancing fool, the energetic clown, right down to Charlton Heston parting the Red Sea with a stroke of his rod—all those wish images and heroic fantasies depend on our sense of American strength and "vigah"—that we could penetrate and conquer the dark virgin wilderness, or come riding into some fierce harlot of a frontier town and, gun in hand, set things right.

For obvious reasons we not only don't believe it any more, we don't feel it, it's no longer part of us.

We have learned that shame and guilt and fear taint our energy and power. That the darkness of the world is huge and can swallow us up. We have become "European." But we haven't accepted it yet. We are frantic in our desire to hide it from ourselves—and that's why the movies have soured and curdled into nonsensical violence, why it's all horror and blood and devils and slaughter. Because we would sooner be annihilated (in fancy) than live within those shameful limits. Because we try to live in our fantasies the opposite of what we fear we are.

The sense that one's powers are limited, that the world sprawls and turns and we are lost in it—a shrinking back toward the simplicities of childhood, the desire to be surrounded by a protective warmth, nostalgia as a symptom of dread.

It's just a thing Max is going through, a symptom of a larger crisis. His wife can't understand it; she sees only the physical manifestation of what is essentially a metaphysical torment.

The world that was is gone, Montgomery Street is gone, and Max's "trouble" is a clue to the going.

He has to learn to live in the mess.

There. The plain simple inevitable messiness of life—that's what bothers him.

Compulsive Max trying to keep his life neat, orderly, patterned, while the world goes to pieces around him.

His last few hairs end up tangled in a hairbrush. Doors stick. The roof leaks. He's always fumbling for keys. He steps in dogshit, can't quite get the last dab of it off his shoe. That dead cat in the gutter, the stench of it—"Why don't they come and cart it away?" His memory of the splatter of the old lady's brains on the sidewalk. The black stains of old melted wax in front of the candy store. The grime of the subway. The black woman in the pink kimono, her disarrayed hair, her smeared-on lipstick, the thought of her stained and sweat-soaked bed, of pillowcases smeared with Dixie Peach pomade. His wife is no housekeeper. The bathroom sink grimy with dried soap and spots of toothpaste. Unwashed dishes. Rotting food in the refrigerator. Moldy bread.

"This place is becoming a goddam sty!"

"You don't like it? Clean it yourself!"

In his store, a pile of some kind, stacked tins of antique furniture polish, suddenly tumble—the vibrations of the buses going by! Entropy. The sense of his own body aging, softening, beginning to rot. Sweat, the fierce heat of the day. "Mister, get the ball!" Picks it up but can't quite get it back over the fence into the schoolyard; walks away rubbing his arm. The scratch on his head. A kid at play falling, scraping his knee. Torn flesh, ooze of blood—a close-up of it can be more devastating than an ax murder.

His shoelaces keep coming untied; hopping around on one leg trying to fix them. He puts his cigar down into a can of paste or paint instead of into the ashtray. "I read somewhere you lose twenty thousand brain cells a day." "Is that right? Where do they go?" His memory seems to be failing. "I was going to say something but I forget what it is." "Max, you're not old enough yet to be senile!"

At lunchtime, the bread of his sandwich crumbles, meat and mustard come spilling out.

The gun is just another part of the mess; the way it just turns up, blank, anomalous, a sign of the randomness of things. The threat of violence implicit throughout. Two burly black men in a bashed car park in front of his store—he's sure they're planning to rob him. Kill or be killed. "You're going to Brownsville? I wouldn't go into that jungle!" Death is the ultimate dissolution of form, the final mess.

The storm. Max gets caught in it, soaked. Sewers overflowing. Sodden garbage floating in the gutters.

Overplay these things and you end up with slapstick. Underplay it, then, keep it subordinated to other actions. It's the texture of life and there's not a damn thing you can do about it.

You combat the mess by building Montgomery Streets, by structuring life rigidly. Laws and rules. Thou Shalt Nots. The aura of police stations and synagogues and a nagging conscience. Max comes close to submitting to these. But he also struggles against them. Stevie, spooked by the mess of freedom, passes into the sanctity and order of the place; he will do his dance in the circle; this is implicit in the Anita scene. Max, having lived within that drab order all his life, now yearns to break out.

The gun focuses that yearning.

It terrifies him. Fear, damnable fear, the essence of Montgomery Street, the fear that draws a tight circle around itself like a wagon train fending off an attack of Indians.

Mother to her little boy: "Stop acting like a wild Indian!"

"Come down from there before you break your neck!"

"You're going to poke someone's eye out with that thing!"

It's potency that Max is afraid of. The fear that if you break through the limits of self, of habit, obsession, caution, order, marriage, community, you might become part of the mess. The fear that freedom is a nightmare, all dissonance, dissipation, demons, death.

Why?

Maybe I have to posit in Max's past a trauma, a moment of bitter insight, a nightmare vision. The old lady jumping off the roof? No, it has to be more than that, worse than that. Something that drove him to Montgomery Street, to his desire for limits, boundaries, order, formal control—something that trimmed his ambitions, soured his dreams—some fact in his life that will correlate to the inexplicable obsessions of mine.

A love that died horribly, absurdly, when he was young? Emblem of a burned-out romanticism. A moment of brutal violence—he saw his father murdered by hoodlums?

A child that died? Photograph of a sweet-faced little boy on the night table?

They were preoccupied with something else—sex?—thus their marriage is tainted with accusations, unspoken despair.

No.

I'm feeling hollowed out, as empty and futile as a used paper cup. The sense I've had ever since coming home of having been violated—that burglary, I suppose. The sanctity of home, the sanctity of self, entered and defiled.

The things we hold on to, for no good reason at all, it seems.

But there has to be a reason. There just has to be.

———

I suppose it's because, for once, I'm copying so much from life. It's a kind of stealing—and I have to wonder what holes I'm leaving in my sense of the past. How will the Montgomery Street I am inventing alter the remembered life of the Montgomery Street I knew? I used to feel that I was adding something to the world, an artifact, a bit of entertainment, an idea or two—a length of film. But with this thing there's that sense of taking something away, grabbing a chunk of what was once vivid and solid and reducing it to a bunch of shadows cast on a screen. The cliché is that art enriches reality; true, I suppose. But it can impoverish it, too. Does that explain this meager feeling, this sickness at heart?

Or am I only parading before myself, showing off my simple worries—mostly commerical—as though they were profound regrets.

The furtive pleasure I'm feeling right now, writing this. The way I treasure my moments of despair. The way I was taught to punish myself in anticipation of pleasures to come.

———

I've managed to explain it to her, perhaps more clearly than I ever could have explained it to myself. "Your trouble," she said, "is that you are trying to create it and exorcise it at the same time. You want to go back to it, because it's ultimately where you live, but you're afraid of losing what you've managed to accomplish, of reducing yourself down to what you were when you were there." Which I suppose in the way of analysis is as good as any. My good doctor, my sympathetic darling! "You're afraid that to show it the way it was is to betray it, but you're too goddam stubborn to pretty it up. Tell me the truth: was it really so awful?"

Well, was it?

———

If he isn't impotent and he isn't a cuckold, what's left? Where's the story?

Shut up tight. Images won't come. Familiar enough pattern. I've gotten too close to it. Need distance. I'm not sure what I've accomplished or what remains to be done. Ground out, anyway, last night, an outline for Z. Blurred the problems, skirted the holes. Maybe some feedback will help.

The gray realities of the place. How it seemed to me, living there, smaller than life, less than life. Going to the movies as a way of living somewhere else. The way life seems to exist always in the future or the past, never right here and now. In that sense, we all live on Montgomery Street, and to film it is a redundancy. Unless it be transformed. But that isn't what I set out to do. Drab realities make drab films. Can you count on the energy of actors to undermine the listlessness of the parts they play?

Why do I keep remembering Korski, and that atrocious secret he kept hidden up his sleeve? And his dim wife, munching her Kaiser roll with its thick slab of butter, barricading herself behind the inexorable armor of fat and meanness. For God's sake, what were they ashamed of? Why guilt?—when they might have been expected to flaunt the tattoo of their martyrdom and survival as a badge of honor.

Surviving. But what, in fact, besides the blatancy of physical outrage and death, did they survive?

The depravity of the Nazis, the dreary platitude that man is a beast, the blank horror at the heart of things—sure. But certainly the very fact that we are free to be beasts means that we are also free to be gods. Nightmares are just the underside of our most paradisiacal dreams.

The blank horror—blank, blankness.

The way they were stripped of everything—their clothes,

145

their hair, their false teeth and glass eyes, their homes, their books, their families, their customs and ceremonies, their past, their future, the very structure of their selves; the horror that must have come in that bizarre sense of freedom—how they must have seen that we are nothing but a tangle of secondary characteristics—they were nothing, and life was nothing, and still, stupidly, absurdly, with self-loathing, they lived, they went on living. It's that nothingness we most fear.

Bestiality, violence, torn and dead flesh, these are frightening. But far more frightening is the knowledge of artifice, of illusion, of how we make our lives up out of memories of the past and dreams of the future and so avoid the blank and absolute nothingness of the present moment—the invisible, impossible Now—

Max has inklings of some of this. He was there, he saw the camps. His platoon liberated Buchenwald—he was assigned to interview the survivors—he understands. And that's why he fled to Montgomery Street, that's why he fenced himself in, that's why he concocted a life out of artifacts, soap carvings, the slapstick conventions of marriage, clung to his past, surrendered his future. Because, finally, he knows that he is nothing more than a shadow cast by a world of his own making, insubstantial, transient, a flicker on a screen. He has no core, he is nothing but surface, style is all!

———

Drove upstate yesterday with J. Her idea. She just had to see the trees in flame color, the ritual of fall. We went up along the Taconic and she sat next to me, cooing and exulting like a little girl, while I, feeling a bit like Max, tried to feign enthusiasm. "It's just absolutely gorgeous, isn't it?" "Sure." Eventually, inevitably, my sourness curdled everything. Ate a dismal lunch in a road-house above Poughkeepsie, all lagging conversation and too much salt and a lingering taste of ashes in the wine. Talked about the project. Tried to imply the limits of her role. Drove back to

Manhattan in drizzle and gloom. She's really very nice about things. I had to keep refusing an invitation to "come in."

I confess I am deriving a certain wry pleasure from it, the role I have fallen into, the way I am being courtly and scrupulous and "hard to get." The understanding between us, the joy of the game, the tingle of knowing we will eventually arrive at the end of it.

Z called. He's read the outline. "It's good, there's something solid there, but I see a problem or two. Let's come together and talk about it. Shall we say tomorrow?" Fine.

Sometimes I astonish myself. For example, I slept peacefully last night. For example, I rose up out of bed this morning feeling fresh and cocky and strong. For example, I don't seem to care at all what Z is going to say.

Z's office. Z behind his desk. Mort in the big leather chair looking like death warmed over, not quite willing to meet my eyes. I want this all on paper. I want to treasure it forever. Oscar and his twin brother, freshly polished just to impress me, peered down at all of us from Z's trophy case, along with all the cups and blue ribbons won by Z's famous dogs. Outside, behind a double thickness of glass, a crisp October afternoon, a glorious sun-speckled day. I'm still a bit high from the afterglow of it. Handshakes. A sense of conspiracy in the air. Eyebeams scattering around the room, trying not to tangle. We just didn't know— did we?—what we had planned for each other. An odd formality that ought to have set my teeth on edge but mysteriously didn't. I collapsed into the big white sofa, challenging its hideous softness to overwhelm me, feeling a bit like some hard-bitten kid sent down to see the principal for heaving a hunk of chalk at the teacher. "Yeah, you wanted to see me, what's it all about?"

We chatted. We discussed the election. We drank coffee. We

147

stalled. It seems the party wasn't yet complete. Z had invited along a fellow named Irving. Irving is a script doctor. Irving is making himself quite a reputation in the trade. I had to confess I had never heard of him, but Irving, of course, knows all about me. Z had given him a copy of the outline. Irving has a few suggestions. Is that right? "Look, I don't know what he's going to say. All I'm asking is that you keep an open mind."

Enter Irving, all professional smile. My age, my height— Irving, my brother. A sense of scalps hanging from his Gucci belt and credit cards bulging his Gucci wallet. That air of cool enthusiasm that is exhaled by a clever, unperturbable mind. A handshake that invites you to step outside if you don't like it. You will never hear Irving confess he spent a restless night.

Irving was happy to meet me. He thought *Centerpiece* was a "terrific" piece of work, a "winner." I became aware that my teeth had begun to ache.

To business.

First of all (this, more or less, is Irving talking) I want you to know that I love, I really love, the Brooklyn angle. Local color, *ambiance*, the possibility of a nice gritty *mise en scène*, I like it, it's good stuff. Besides, it's where we all come from, isn't it? And I do like Stevie, the theme of initiation, coming of age, that's the great American story, isn't it?

Sure it is!

But—I was waiting for the but—but, says Irving, as I was telling Toby here, the rest of it, to be quite honest with you, lacks something. Impact. There just doesn't seem to be enough happening. Frinstance: you have here a character who finds a gun, which is fine, nice, a grabber. But the question is, what do you do with it? Be a good citizen, turn it in at the police station? Is he supposed to be Andy Hardy's father or something? I remember Chekhov saying, never introduce a gun that doesn't go off. So, right off the bat, I think that gun just has to be fired.

Fine, said I, keeping an open mind, whom shall we shoot?

148

The wife, of course. And that's where we have to think about making some drastic changes.

I look at Mort, Mort looks at Z, Z looks at Irving, and Irving, as though he was performing a magic trick, lights a slim black cigar.

"Shall I continue?"

"Just listen to him," says Z. "It never hurts to have a fresh point of view."

I said I was all ears.

Okay, then. Insofar as Irving can deduce from what is, after all (smile), just a sketchy outline, I tend to view the wife sympathetically. Now what he would do ("and remember, all I'm doing is offering suggestions") is to make her bitchy, utterly bitchy. The point is that she ought to deserve to be shot. You want to get the audience on Max's side, make them want to shoot her themselves.

Do go on.

To start with, she actually seduces Stevie. You can see how that adds some meat to his part in the story. Of course, he's only fourteen, a little too young for the plot—but does it really change much if we make him sixteen? But wait, that's just a side issue. The real key to it is that we make her an absolute fanatic about women's lib, an ultrafeminist, a real ball-buster. What we're talking about here is injecting a little controversy, something topical, something that people can come out of the theater arguing about.

"I'll be frank with you, Stephen"—how about if we shoot Irving?—"I think you've got a nice little story here, a few laughs, a few tears, which is fine, which is good, but I just don't see it as the kind of thing that's going to drag them away from their television. Nowadays you've got to reach out and grab 'em and yank 'em into the goddam theater."

Among the things I learned about myself this afternoon is that I am idiotically polite. Instead of braining Irving with an Oscar, I

149

merely suggested, quite mildly, that I couldn't recall much of a feminist movement back in 1960, not in Brooklyn anyway. But that didn't faze him. After all, that the picture takes place in 1960 isn't absolutely crucial to the plot. Besides, it costs money to do a period piece. You have to go rent all those old cars. Here, of course, a glance at Z.

It went on for quite a while, but enough, enough. In the end he had a dangerous and demented Max holding Stevie hostage, and the air was filled with sirens and tear gas and breaking windows, and it was all happening, Irving's nightmare, not in Brooklyn—"I mean, after all, who the hell lives in Brooklyn nowadays?"—but out on the Island somewhere, let's say Lake Success, and the wife was a corpse, and the time was the present, and everything—everything!—was torn, ruined, dead.

Then he was gone. Or rather he seemed to vanish back into the void from which Z had conjured him, and it was just the three of us again, having a drink, all buddy-buddy, and rather glum.

"Okay," I said. "Do we make Irving's movie or mine?"

He surprised me, he really did. A look of gloomy hurt and indecision came over his face, and he said, without the slightest hint of conviction, "So maybe Irving goes too far, but at least his instincts are commercial."

And that's when it happened. Ten years ago I would have called it an epiphany. Six months ago I would have thought I was losing my mind. But it was marvelous and magical, a kind of Alice-in-Wonderlandish feeling, with a hint of music playing in my ears and the sensation of coming out of a dream. The feeling that I was growing into a giant, that I towered over them, that I could pick them up, one in each hand, and shake them until they howled, and set them down on a shelf. Mort, however, was a triviality. It focused on Z. Toby the Terrible had become, once and for all, Toby the Meek. It was a question of who was to be master—that's all. And I know he sensed it, too.

"Just tell me one thing," he said. "Do you know what you're doing?"

"Absolutely."

"Then fine. I just wanted to be sure."

I'm sitting here, still tingling, still feeling incomprehensibly blithe and clearheaded and huge, as though my footsteps could shake the neighborhood, thinking: I've done it, I've come through it, I've come through. The world is my playground; let us go celebrate; it's my picture now!

Took J to Elaine's. First time ever I didn't feel intimidated. Is it only a mood? How long will it last? You, squeamish Stevie, silence your qualms. Went to a movie afterward, sat in the back row, and giggling, parodying ourselves, we necked. Then the only problem was whose apartment to return to. The act itself, pleasurable enough, seemed nonetheless anticlimactic, symbol, perhaps, of the loss of youth. We have already moved beyond being lovers in the technical sense to something more permanent. She's out right now collecting some "things" she just can't live without, moving herself over here. "At least we'll pretend it's permanent," is what she said, "give ourselves a chance." I liked having her here this morning, the way she seemed to fill the place up. I liked watching her scowl at my meager pantry while she prepared a shopping list. I love her litheness, so unlike the dead-weight feeling of E, her legs around me, that sense of a fluid and perfect fit. I love playing Yin and Yang with her. I love seeing her "undies" pale pink and freshly washed like the gossamer of Paradise drying on my towel rack. Corny? So what? I am that sort of man.

The trouble is that I kept thinking I had to have a plot for Max, something happening, some "big" action filled with "meaning." I was as bad as Irving. I gave him the gun and then I was stuck because I didn't know what to have him do with it. Because the

151

gun implies plot, story, and that's not really what I'm interested in. The shape of it, the sense of it, must come through the collision of images. A movie is nothing more than a lot of "bits" of film juxtaposed in an interesting way. The juxtaposition is everything. Max and Stevie, Stevie and Max, each scene relating to each. And the background, the murmuring and crucial life of Montgomery Street, retrieved from nonexistence, made lasting, vivid, real.

So forget the gun. He doesn't find it. It doesn't exist and never has. It's not a "big" day for him, it's just another day. He works, he laughs, he goes on: that's all there is to it. Because Max isn't the point of the thing. He's just a prism through which we can view a moment of life caught in a moment of time. Which is enough.

Funny. Keep it funny. Not plot but scene is the crux of it. Not story but the hidden weaving of images.

Can I get away with it, excising the narrative conventions? I sure can try.

———

Max waking up. That bathroom scene more or less as is, the whirl of his brown sputum in the vortex of a grungy sink. A scene with his wife, the way he indulges her. Maybe she likes to read the morning paper—or, better, have breakfast in bed. His ambivalence as he pampers her. Stevie running outside. Sees him through the window, makes him wistful: if only I had a kid like that. Maybe they should meet, come together in the end. Think about it. Dresses, clamps a cigar into his mouth, big and fat and brown, none of Irving's stogy crap. Goes down to buy some donuts, a newspaper. Runs into the neighbor who's going to have the heart attack. Where? Steps, street, candy store? The old guy is tramping upstairs with a bag of rolls and milk, wheezing, rubbing his chest.

"Oscar, you all right, Oscar? You don't look so well."

"It's the heat!"

Keep it—

Why not let the old man be Stevie's father?

That's how they come together in the end, a long scene for the two of them in the hospital waiting room. Will the old man die? While Ellie back home is taking care of Stevie's hysterical mom.

Stevie the son Max never had; Max the "good" father Stevie desires. Too easy? It seems right. So long as I keep the irony up.

They come together, they meet, they spend a long anxious night together, but they never quite break through to each other. The poignancy of it, the inarticulation of Montgomery Street; the impossibility of ever unearthing your own deepest roots. Hold it at a distance—the challenge of keeping the tone intact.

The nagging sense that it's too familiar, that I've heard it somewhere before, the sense that I'm sitting here rather giddily and nonchalantly inventing someone else's story. Ah, I remember. Never mind, do it anyway. Artists steal.

Stevie's father near the doorway, gray jacket, brown pants, paint-spattered shoes, chalky skin. The big slab of him standing stiff and erect, against a wall. Max comes through the big glass door.

M: What are you doing there, Oscar—holding up the building?

O (friendly but humorless): I'm standing.

M: I see you're standing. How come you're not working today?

O: I'm allowed to take a day off.

M: You picked a good one. So what are you going to do—stand there all day?

O: What's to do? I'll walk to the park.

He seems to be in pain, sternly held in.

M (no longer bantering, authentically concerned): What's the matter, Oscar? You look a little green around the gills.

O (throwaway motion that becomes the familiar ancient

153

shrug): *Gar nicht,* something I ate.

M: Maybe you should see a doctor.

O: Listen to that. You and my wife. What do I wanna see a doctor for? So he should poke around in me and give me pills and tell me what I shouldn't eat? Doctors I don't need. Quacks, the bunch of them. I say when your time comes, it comes, and you're done with it.

M: Suit yourself. (Bantering again.) Me, I plan to live forever.

O: Then good luck to you. (Without a change of tone.) It's supposed to be a hot one today.

M: So they said.

O: So what are you going to do? Sit in your store and swelter?

M: Do I have a choice? I'll see you later.

Another angle. Takes a step. Along comes Benny, rather jaunty, whistling his song.

M: Hello, Benny! You're awfully chipper this morning.

B: Why not, Max?

Benny goes by.

Crosses the street, goes into the grocery as Stevie emerges from the candy store. We pick up Stevie, etc.

———

Give Stevie a morning scene with his father? "Why do you have to run? Why do you have to get all overheated in this weather?"

"Awr, leave me alone!"

"Don't you open a mouth to me, *boychik.*"

Sullen Stevie, inarticulate Oscar: how they never could say to each other the things they needed to hear.

"When I'm dead and buried I'll leave you alone."

———

Max in the candy store, Bertie and Willy having at one another, arguing about money. They try to drag him in as an arbiter.

"I'm asking you, Max. She orders forty dollars' worth of model airplanes. The kids around here love model airplanes, she tells me. The markup is forty percent, she tells me. So look at

154

them, here they sit. Because who the hell wants to buy model airplanes in a candy store? The hobby shop on Nostrand Avenue, that's where you buy model airplanes, not in a goddam candy store. The only way we'll ever get rid of the damn things is if they fly away on their own."

And Bertie: "And you should fly away with them! Mister Bigmouth over there."

"Shut up, you crazy bitch! And then if I put a couple of bucks on a sure thing, she lets me have it."

"A couple of bucks? Who are you kidding, a couple of bucks! It's a sickness with you, Willy! Tell him, Max. From me he won't listen."

Max: Please, Bertie. All I want is a couple of Antony and Cleopatras.

Willy: You see? You see? Cigars we can sell, Hershey bars we can sell, newspapers we can sell—but we can't sell goddam model airplanes!

B: Lower your voice, Willy. The whole neighborhood doesn't have to hear.

W: Let them hear! What? It's a secret nobody knows? It's a secret? You've got them out there in the goddam window, you imbecile, you!

Max finally gets his cigars and leaves.

———

Max in the kitchen, cooking breakfast, the same sort of fried eggs Stevie will eat. Furious at himself when he breaks a yolk. Newspaper propped up so he can read while he works. Headlines, movie ads. Brings coffee to his wife. Wakes her up gently.

E: So what's new in the world today?
M: What's ever new?
E: Listen, you'll stop at the bank today and get some cash?
M: Again? I gave you cash on Wednesday.
E: It's gone.
M: How could it be gone?

155

E: I spent it, that's how it could be gone.

M: For God's sake, Ellie!

Sure. Not death, not murder and suicide, not impotence, not chaos, but money, cash, moola, dough, that was the obsession of Montgomery Street. Where's the next dollar coming from? How are we going to pay the rent? You know what it costs to send a kid to college these days? I'd love a new car, but who can afford it? The whole crazy litany. Make it a kind of chorus, voices in the background.

"I work hard for my money and you spend it like water!"

"Could you lend me a ten till Monday?"

"What? You think it's not just as easy to fall in love with a rich girl?"

"If I'd listened to him then, I'd be living on Easy Street."

Money as freedom, the only freedom that meant much, the only freedom they knew.

"He had a bankroll on him would choke a horse."

"Would you believe a shnook like that ends up a millionaire?"

"You want to live in this world, here's what it takes"—the hand up, the thumb rubbing across the first two fingers.

In the *shul* they charge you for seats for the holidays. A cop comes into Max's store for his weekly *shmear*. "You don't pay off, the next thing you know you've got fourteen building violations."

The street is drenched with thoughts of money. It's what's on Max's mind that day. With his wife: she wants to go away for the weekend, but they can't afford it. His landlord comes into the store for the rent and Max has to beg for more time. Tries to get a loan from someone. Give Ellie a successful brother. The humiliation of it. Adds an edge to the Brownsville scene.

Stevie's father has been "laid off."

"You collecting unemployment at least?"

"Sure I'm collecting. But it's no way to live. When I first came to this country—look, I'll show you something—"

Reaches into his pocket, shows Max that gold coin.

"It was the only money I had, but did I spend it? I had gold in my pocket and I went hungry! I'm stubborn that way. I'll die with it in my pocket and then my Stevie will have it."

His head bobbing up and down; tight on his chalky face, his damp eyes.

"I don't want he should say I never left him nothing."

Have him give Stevie the coin on the way to the hospital? No, that's an Irving. Just plant it in the morning and leave it alone.

————

Max's brother-in-law is also an antique dealer; has a posh "boutique" on Madison Avenue. He put Max into the business. He's the antithesis of Ellie: Republican, lives in Larchmont, drives a Caddy, wife and kids. Some kind of fight between them years back. They despise each other, haven't even talked to each other for months. Max has to call him up for a loan—maybe he can't let Ellie know.

They arrange to meet at an antique auction uptown.

A scene with the landlord, an old Jew in a long black coat and white beard. Max blustering his way through it.

"Don't worry, Mr. Ginzberg. If I tell you you'll have your money next week, believe me, you'll have it."

Ginzberg's shrewd eyes, calculating the value of Max's stock.

Then Max struggling with himself, finally making the phone call.

In the end the brother-in-law gives him the money because he loves the thought of his sister needing him.

————

Max on his way to the auction goes down into the subway, just missing the train Stevie and Lester take to Chinatown. Play with the number of times they almost meet.

Maybe have Willy come to Max for a loan. Gives him five dollars.

The auction scene. Not too fancy. A meeting hall, bridge chairs, pieces of old furniture spread around the walls. Clusters of lamps, vases, glassware, dishes on tables near the front. Mirrors reflecting segments of the whole. Antique-dealer types: women with bleached blond hair done up in "beehives" and too much make-up, fanning themselves with catalogues and nattering about "deals." Slightly shabby men, not much different from Max. As he moves through the place, looking for his brother-in-law, he keeps running into people he knows.

"Max Stein! How the hell are you? Haven't seen you in a dog's age. You still out there in Brooklyn?"

He gets patted on the back, his hand is grabbed, the easy familiarity of the trade, people touching him.

"Hey, Maxie, how would you like to have half a dozen corn planters? You know, corn planters, real ones. I'll let you have 'em cheap. I've got a dozen of the things and I'll never move them all."

"How's the missus, Maxie? Still keeping you up nights?"

The camera follows him through the crowd.

"Hi, Shirley. Hi, Lily. Good to see you, Manny. Fine, Sammy, and how's by you?"

"Did you hear about Leo, Max?"

"Hear what?"

"The poor bastard's in the hospital."

"That's too bad. Serious?"

"Cancer in the gut."

This from an older man, smirking as he tells it, that satisfaction that comes from outlasting your contemporaries.

Snatches of conversation emerge from the hubbub.

"So I told him, I said, if that's a Louie fourteen then my name is Marie Antoinette."

"She's a beaut, she is. For half a buck she'd step on your face."

"Wisconsin, he tells me. Wisconsin? I say. You want it shipped to Wisconsin, that costs extra!"

"Sure, sure, that and fifteen cents will get you on the subway."

"If he thinks he's gonna run my life, he's got another think coming."

"He tells me it's pure Ukbar. Who's he trying to kid?"

A horse-faced woman with a neighing laugh. A little guy, self-absorbed, adding figures on a scrap of paper, hating the world around him. An enormous fat man occupying two seats. A mannish dark-haired woman trying to soothe a diaphanous blond girl who seems on the verge of tears. Someone laughing hysterically. Someone else doing a slow burn. A bearded man who seems to become aware of the camera and, for an instant, peers out at us.

"Hey, let's grab a seat, they're starting."

From Max's POV we see a dapper man sitting alone in the back row. He wears a pearly gray suit, a shirt with a gold stickpin through the collar, a silk tie, stylishly narrow. Hair combed back and slicked down. A whiff of expensive cologne. Fancy gold cufflinks visible. He sees Max, nods faintly. He's a quiet, self-contained, snobbish little guy, a contrast to the loud gesticulating types we've just seen. He's more used to those fancy Fifth Avenue auctions where it's all done with a wink and a nod. He holds himself aloof from the raucous life around him, the sense that if he gets too close to it, he'll sully his manicured fingertips.

Max sits down next to him. The auction starts up in the background.

M: Hello, Irving.

I: So? You need money?

M: I haven't said that yet.

I: I don't hear from you for months, then you call me up out of the blue. Don't play games with me, Max. Just tell me how much.

M (ashamed): Three hundred. Just for a week or two. You know how dead business is in the summer.

A beat.

I: So how is she?

M: She's fine. We're both fine. And by you?

I: No complaints. My Sheila is flying off to London tomorrow. She's gonna study the harpsichord, of all things. Can you imagine?

M: She's going alone?

I: I'm supposed to stop her? Aah, kids. (Pause.) So what's happening with you, Max? When are you going to get yourself the hell out of Brooklyn?

M: I like Brooklyn.

I: You like Brooklyn. I like Brooklyn. But in Brooklyn you don't make a living, Max.

Auctioneer in the background: I've got ten, I've got ten, who'll give me fifteen, fifteen, fifteen, fifteen . . .

I: Look at the garbage they're selling. They're gonna nickel and dime us to death. What'd you do to your head?

Max fingers the scratch. Waves a hand.

M: Bumped it. What are you doing here, Irving? I thought this was below your class.

I: Gotta keep up. (Knowing smile.) Look over there, what do you see?

Intercut: some rugs draped casually over some chairs. One of them has a deep-blue pattern in it.

M: Rugs.

I: That's why you come to me for money. You see rugs. But

you don't know rugs. I know rugs, Max. Now, you see the blue one. It's an old Artzukhan. And how is it listed in the catalogue—Persian! A lot they know, huh?

Auctioneer: I've got forty once, I've got forty twice, and—sold!

I: Forty bucks for a piece of carnival glass. That's not business, it's just gambling. So you need three hundred? Okay, I'll give you three hundred. (Takes out a checkbook.) You want I should make it five hundred? I mean, blood is blood, you don't have to be ashamed to ask.

M (containing anger): Three hundred will be fine.

Irving writes the check.

I: You told her you were doing this?

M: No.

I (with emotion): Well, then you tell her, you hear me, Max? You tell her she has a brother, you hear me? Let her know she owes me. It'll do her good. Here.

Gives him the check. Max puts it in his pocket. We watch the blue rug auctioned off. Irving doesn't bid. It's sold to a youngish handsome woman for $675.

Max (surprised): But I thought—

I (big supercilious grin): My associate. A nice girl, real nice.

She looks at Irving and smiles, a hint of intimacy.

The auctioneer, then cut to Stevie in Chinatown.

Max huddled in the doorway of a shop. The downpour. Cops in yellow slickers. People running. A young couple, arm in arm, soaking wet, loving every minute of it.

Stevie's day is a bit too full, Max's a touch too empty. But never mind. The point is the contrast, the balance, the way they come together.

Or rather the way, in meeting, they fail to come together.

The way literal needs are never satisfied through merely symbolic encounters. The way hungers are only sharpened by a mess of shadows.

———

Memory is to imagination as the sun to the moon.

———

Close-up: a pot of spaghetti sauce simmering, spattering an old stove. Pull back to Ellie trying to adjust the flame, which blinks out. "Damn!" She has to strike a match to turn it on again. In her anger she knocks over a package of spaghetti, the strands tumbling to the floor like a bunch of pick-up-sticks. "Why? Why? Why?" She is on her hands and knees picking the stuff up when we hear a door open and close and Max's voice, with forced cheeriness: "Hello!"

"In the kitchen!"

Another angle as Max enters, dampish and ill at ease.

"I think something's burning."

He adjusts the flame, samples the sauce with a spoon, then gets down to help her.

M: Bad day?

E: Oh, it's been just a terrific day!

This silences him. They finish the job and stand up. She goes on with her cooking while he stands there feeling awkward and guilty.

E: Look, what am I supposed to tell you?

M: Nothing.

A beat or two.

E: I tried to call you before.

M: I had to go uptown.

E: Oh?

M: I saw your brother.

No response. She starts ripping up a lettuce. Her breathing quickens. Finally: So how is he?

On Max: Same as always. He asked about you.

E: That was big of him. Please set the table.

He opens a drawer, starts fumbling with silverware. She breaks spaghetti into a pot of boiling water.

E: How much did he give you?

M: Three hundred.

Tight on her face, the tightness in it, her suppressed reaction.

E: Do you know what I heard today? The Gerofskis are moving.

M: No kidding? Where?

E (shrugging): Where? Out to the Island like everyone else.

M: Idiots!

E (with energy): Sure, idiots! Better they should stay here and rot with the rest of us!

M (stubbornly, but without much conviction): This is still a good place to live.

E (sighs): Max, Max, Max.

M: Don't "Max" me!

E (losing control): Oh, go to hell!

She throws down the lettuce, and runs out of the kitchen. Max stands there a moment, then shuts off the spaghetti sauce, stirs the spaghetti, picks up a piece of lettuce that has fallen to the floor, then follows her. He finds her in the living room, curled up on a chair near the window. He stoops down near her and strokes her hair.

M: Look, I'm sorry. I needed the money and there was no one else to turn to.

E: It's not that. It's—

M: I know, I know.

E (firmly): We've got to get out of here, Max. We've got to get out of this apartment, and off this street, and out of Brooklyn. There's nothing here for us. There never was.

M: You think it will be different someplace else?

E: Yes, I do.

M: Well, I don't. One place is just like another. Where are we going to go? Out to the goddam Island where I'll have a lawn to mow? We don't live out there, Ellie (waving at the window), we live in here (melodramatically thumping his chest).

The camera picks up some of Max's soap figurines. Cut to the schoolyard, the firecracker scene.

Needs work. Time problem. Put it later, just before the heart attack? Have to fill out Max's afternoon and evening, but the holes can be patched in the script. Maybe they should avoid the topic of Irving until later in the evening. It's on Max's mind, gnawing at him, but he's afraid to bring it up. Their fight is interrupted by the heart attack. But it's not really a fight, is it? I seem to sense much more tenderness, much more love between them, than I thought would be there.

Their evening. The kitchen scene, dinner, watching television. He goes down for ice cream, comes back with a "brick" of butter pecan. All of it kept brief, intercut with Stevie's scenes, the schoolyard, the cops, Nellie, Anita.

It doesn't matter. I don't have to put it all down. Because it's coming together now and I know—a knowing that is beyond thoughts and words—that it's going to work.

Stevie in bed, semidarkness, his father coughing. An airplane going by overhead. His mother's voice: "Oscar? What is it, Oscar?" He sits up, listening. A light goes on outside his room. His father gasping. His mother: "Oscar!" Stevie becoming frightened. Have to find a kid who can do it right. No mugging—it has to all be in the eyes.

His parents' bedroom. He comes in in his underwear. His father in pale-blue pajamas, sitting on the edge of the double bed, ghostly white behind the usual chalky white, hand on chest. Croaking noises. His mother already on the verge of hysteria.

S: What's the matter?

Mother: Get him some water!

164

He dashes to the bathroom, fills up a plastic cup.

His mother's voice: What is it, Oscar? Oscar? Oscar!

His father's voice, weakly: I'm all right.

Back to the bedroom with the water. Doesn't know what to do with it. His father seems to be choking, a deep awful terrifying breath.

Mother (falling apart): God help us!

Cut to Max and Ellie. Frantic knocking on the door. They exchange a look. Max opens it to find Stevie in his underwear.

S: It's my father. He's very sick.

Max and Ellie exchange a look of sudden and profound intimacy, a look that dissolves the quarrel between them. They have, after all, through the years, grown subterranean roots together.

They go across the hall to Stevie's apartment.

Don't rush this scene. There can be something almost languid in it, the slowness of reaction time. Oscar, in his stricken state, should seem almost totally self-absorbed, as though he were listening hard to his own inner workings for the faint echoes of reassurance or doom. Stevie in a kind of daze of disbelief, the unreality of it—this can't be happening to me! Max's strength, always implicit, coming out in the emergency. He stoops down at Oscar's side and examines him with all the pseudo assurance of a man who reads medical columns.

M: Can you talk, Oscar? Can you tell me where it hurts? Oscar?

O: I have to go to the bathroom.

M: Don't try to get up.

O: I have to—

He vomits out liquid.

M: Get a towel! (To Ellie.) Call an ambulance!

O: I'm okay. I'm okay.

M: Of course you are. Just lie down here! Come on now. Stevie, you get dressed. You'll have to go down and wait for the ambulance so they won't waste time looking. Go on!

All of it from Stevie's POV. He goes into his bedroom.

His mother's voice: He's dying! God, God, he's dying!

Keep it slow. Stevie's reaction. A minute can seem like an eternity. Listening, fighting back tears, confused. Raises two fists and shakes them. Shakes his head. Pulls himself together and gets dressed. Goes back to the bedroom and sees his father now lying on the bed, breathing heavily, soaked in sweat, Ellie holding his mother.

M (to Ellie): Take her out of here! (Sees Stevie.) Go on down and wait in front of the building. (Stevie doesn't move.) That's the best way to help right now, Stevie.

Stevie goes. Follow him down two flights of stairs and into the dim and tragic street. The long wait: he stands in the gutter, looking for the ambulance. People start looking out of windows. Then Lester is there, comes up to Stevie.

L: Hey, what's happening?

Stevie pays absolutely no attention to him, but starts to cry. Lester, sensitive in the end, shrinks back. The beginnings of a crowd. People murmuring: What is it? I don't know. Someone's sick. It's his father. Tsk-tsk-tsk. What's going on?

Then sirens and the ambulance arriving, the ambulance goons, the irritating and impossible casualness.

S: Please hurry! I'll show you!

He leads them into the building. Linger on the crowd of neighbors, women with housecoats thrown on, some kids, maybe have Bono coming home, heels tapping as he comes down out of the schoolyard to join the scene. The hushed excitement of it. The fear and the pity, the last remnants of community, and above it that macabre pleasure we always felt whenever something happened, anything at all.

The Feuer apartment. The ambulance men getting Oscar onto a stretcher.

M: I'll go with him. Stevie, you'd better stay with your mother.

S: No, I'm going with him.

M: Your mother needs you more right now.

S: I'm going.

E: I'll take care of her. Let him go with you.

He has asserted a right of maturity, and Ellie has recognized it. She is remembering their scene in the morning. They now exchange a look of understanding.

The stretcher going down the staircase—the way you always are afraid they're going to drop the poor bastard.

Again on the crowd as they carry Oscar out. The conversations dying away for a moment.

Then it's the blare of sirens and Brooklyn rushing by and the arrival at the hospital, Oscar snatched away from them, Stevie and Max sent to a waiting room. The drama of the heart attack moves offstage and Stevie and Max, with nothing else to do, are left, finally, to confront each other.

The waiting room is a dreary place with overflowing ashtrays, a tired Coke machine, and public health messages on the walls. The furniture sags with the anxiety and despair of those who have used it. At a desk behind a window a receptionist keeps answering a busy telephone. A security guard, an enormous fat black man. A big round institutional clock—use it to mark the passing of time. One of the walls is glassed and through it we can see the corridor leading to the emergency room. People: three old women dressed in black, Italians or Greeks, taking turns weeping; a well-dressed man who prowls around looking at his watch and pestering the receptionist with unanswerable questions; a rabbinical type who is fast asleep. Others come and go through the long night—make them vaguely recapitulate the events of the day.

Stevie sitting on the edge of a chair, head down, hands

clasped between his legs, examining the floor. Max across from him, watching him with concern and tenderness. The camera moves slowly around them, a long tracking shot in which nothing happens at all.

Max, finally: He'll be all right.

Gets no response.

M: They can do marvelous things nowadays. (Still no response.) He was still conscious when they took him in. That's a good sign.

Stevie lifts his head, as though it weighed a thousand pounds, and slowly nods, without conviction.

M: Wanna Coke?

Stevie's shoulders go up and down.

A beat. Then Max stands up and goes to the Coke machine. He puts a coin in. No cup falls; through the little plastic window we can see the stuff pour down and vanish through the grating. Max slaps the machine, as though to punish it, is about to accept the loss, then starts fiddling. Max the fix-it man, undaunted by technology. He manages somehow to wriggle his hand up into the machine and pull a cup down. He puts another coin in. A second cup falls into the first and fills. Max, satisfied, takes both cups, shares the Coke between them, and carries them back to Stevie.

S: Thanks.

He takes a cup, gulps it down. Max hands him the second cup.

S: No thanks.

M: Go on, have it.

Stevie accepts.

Max sits down, takes out a cigar, chews off the end, carefully plucks the bit off his tongue and puts it in an ashtray—all the while looking at Stevie, racking his brain for something to say to him, some way to distract him.

M (rather stupidly): He'll be fine.

Stevie glumly nodding.

A resident in surgical dress, looking nonsensically young, like a kid playing doctor, enters. Stevie and Max become alert, but he goes by them and talks to the three women in black. What he tells them seems to cheer them a bit.

On Max's cigar in the ashtray. Dissolve. The cigar has burned down.

Almost as much of a cliché as the clock. Doesn't matter. The whole sequence can be structurally a cliché so long as it is suffused with the particularity of the characters. The fact that it is movieish supplies the necessary distance, keeps it from bathos. Play off throughout the dramatic conventions of film narrative against the nondramatic realities of Montgomery Street. Parody all those rules of movie-making that seem like absolutes. Thwart expectations. A robbery scene without violence. Being chased by a cop but the cop isn't there. A love scene that culminates in a squalid and sloppy kiss. Max getting the money—he doesn't even have to ask. Life as anticlimax. The gun that doesn't go off.

———

We see through the glass a dark young man wearing a windbreaker over an undershirt rushing toward the emergency room carrying an infant wrapped in blankets. A bit later he comes into the waiting room and sits down. He is very distraught.

Max, restless, gets up, stretches. Wanders over to talk to the security guard.

M: Bet you see everything around here.

Guard: You see plenty.

M (indicating the young father): That's about the worst, isn't it? Sick kids.

G (indifferently): It's their own fault. Kid runs a fever, they don't do nothing about it. Then the next thing they know he's gone into convulsions—that's when they bring 'em in. People don't know how to care for their own flesh and blood.

M: The poor guy.

G (a so-what gesture): You surely do see things here. It's quite a show. Half of them sit here chewing their nails and then in the end they walk out smiling. The others—Course this is a private hospital, so you don't get the worst. Now you go across to Kings County, that's where you get to see something. Go in on a Friday, Saturday night, people cut up, shot up, people been in accidents—them's the worst. Yessuh, you surely do see some things.

M: Yeah, I'm sure of it . . . Saw some things myself, during the war.

G: Oh, yeah.

M: Were you in?

G (laughing): I was in. Drove a truck.

M: See much action?

G: Lots of action. Boiled-over radiators. Changing flat tires in the mud.

M (with solemn bravado): I saw some things.

G: Sure. we all saw things. But it's the things you don't see kill you.

Max is helpless in the blare of this cliché.

M: Well—

Awkwardly, he wanders back to Stevie, sits down, rubs his palms dry on his pants.

M: We should be hearing something soon.

S: Yeah. (He yawns.)

M: Why don't you try to take a nap?

S: I'm not tired. (He stifles a yawn.)

M: I think I'll call, see how your mother is holding up.

Stevie nods.

Max calls E from a pay phone. Split screen?

M: It's me.

E: Any word yet?

170

M: We're still waiting it out. How is she?

E: I had my hands full with her, but I finally got her to take one of my pills and she fell asleep.

M: It's such a goddam shame.

E: Max, I love you.

M: Mm. I know. Me too.

E: How's Stevie taking it?

M: He's working hard at being a man about it. Poor kid.

E: It's going to be roughest for him.

M: Yeah.

E: Maybe it will all work out.

M: Sure. Everything always works out. Listen, I'll see you later.

E: I'm going to try to sleep.

M: Good idea. S'long.

Returns to Stevie.

M: Don't worry about her. She's okay.

S: Thanks.

Sits down. Time passes.

Stevie gets up, walks around reading the public health messages. The warning signs of cancer. Smoking can kill you. How to recognize VD. Returns to Max.

M: It should be soon now.

S (rather calmly): He's going to die, isn't he?

M (with the bluntness that comes in the small hours of the morning): I don't know, Stevie. It's taking a long time.

S: Even if he doesn't die, he won't be able to work.

M: Not for a while.

S: What am I going to do?

M: He must have insurance.

S: I don't mean about money. About my mother.

M: Well—

S: You saw what she was like. She was like crazy. I mean, that my father is sick—okay, he's sick. And if he dies, well, he dies.

171

But my mother was like a crazy woman. I couldn't do anything for her. That's what bothered me most of all.

Max doesn't know what to say.

S: It's awful. But that's all I've been thinking about. My mother. I'm afraid she'll—

M: She'll what?

S: She won't be able to live without him. She'll—

M: You'll have to help her.

S: What can I do?

M: People do what they have to do.

Stevie shakes his head.

M: You're going to do your growing up real fast now.

S (tremendously agitated): It stinks. It just stinks!

M: Listen. You got family. You got neighbors. People come through in the end. It's not like you live somewhere where nobody knows anyone else. You'll see.

S (bitterly): There's nothing to see.

They are distracted momentarily by the phone ringing.

S (stiffly): I'm sorry. I know you're trying to make me feel better.

M: So what do you want? That I should make you feel worse?

Stevie, dimly, smiles.

More time passing.

––––––––

S: I was an accident, you know.

M (amused): Is that right?

S: They didn't want kids. They were already in their forties when they had me.

M: Maybe they just couldn't afford you earlier.

S: No, I was an accident. I just happened to come along.

––––––––

M: How much you get paid working for Korski?

S: Seventy-five an hour.

M: So that's not so bad for a kid your age.

S: Now you sound like my father.

The gloom, which has momentarily lifted, returns.

———

M: Want another Coke?

S: I've already got to pee something awful.

M: So go pee.

S: I can wait.

M: Hey. Go pee. I'll stay here while you're gone.

S: I don't know where it is.

M: Then ask.

Stevie, embarrassed, asking the security guard for the men's room.

———

Stevie sleeping. Max putting his jacket over him?

———

Doctor enters. Max and Stevie get up as he approaches.

M: Well?

Doc: He's stabilized.

S: Is he—

The doctor ignores Stevie, talks only to Max.

Doc: The crisis is past, for now. There's nothing more you can do for him tonight. Tomorrow we'll do some tests, and then we'll see. Why don't you take the boy home?

S (almost angry): I want to see him.

M: Can we go up?

Doc: He's sleeping.

S: Look, I want to see him.

The doctor finally looks at Stevie.

Doc: Okay, just for a minute. I'll arrange it.

———

Oscar in an oxygen tent, hooked up to machines, looking terribly old and on the verge of death. Stevie peering down at his father, something hard and final and resigned in his eyes. Max fascinated for a moment by the proximity of all the gadgets.

M: You'll see tomorrow, it'll all be different.

S: But he looks so awful.

M: You'll see.

S: Sure.

He touches the clear plastic with a finger.

M: Come on, let's go home.

The camera follows them back out into the corridor, past a night nurse on duty, bored, indifferent, reading a movie magazine and scratching a tooth with a long fingernail. A moment of waiting by an elevator. The door opens, they step into the elevator and out onto Montgomery Street.

———

Let the final shot echo the first. It is dawn. The camera tracks them as they come down Montgomery Street, pass, then we watch their receding backs. There are cats at play among garbage cans. No bagpipes, but on the sound track the echo of the tune the bagpipes had played. Yellow light in a window blinking on. A newspaper truck goes by, stopping for a moment at the candy store to toss out the daily bundles. The camera begins to rise slowly as Max puts an arm around Stevie's shoulder and Stevie shrugs it off. They are small figures far below as they enter their apartment building. The camera continues to rise until we are high above looking down through a rosy dawn at the gray and slumbering sprawl of Brooklyn. Freeze it, and the end credits roll.

———

Toby called. When does he see a script? When do we start casting? If I want Gordie Auger on cameras we have to go into production in April Then Mort. Can I come by to sign some papers? How about lunch? How's the script going? Then J. She can have a two-week job on the Coast if she doesn't mind taking her clothes off. How do I feel about it? Well, how *do* I feel about it? These last couple of weeks have been a kind of heaven, but I can't expect it to last. *Centerpiece* opens here tomorrow. Preview reactions have been mixed. Tuesday I'm scheduled for the *Tonight* show to puff it. How do I avoid telling them that it's all ancient history for me? Well, you see, Johnny, the public is always one movie behind me; I live with the one I'm making next. The games we play. And I'm still not satisfied with Max. Never mind. Stevie's fine, and I've gotten to the heart of the thing, the street, the neighbors, the air of the place, the bricks and sidewalks and dirty windows, the sounds and the smells, I'll have all that—the buildings, the garbage, the faces, the feel of it, the texture of it, it's come to life for me, I can see it now. The rest will be easy.